LOCKED DOWN BY HOOD LOVE

2

BY LATOYA NICOLE

D1519209

DEDICATION

TO KENDRICK "KOJACK" EDWARDS,

YOU CAN'T EVEN IMAGINE THE VOID YOU LEFT IN MY HEART. WE HAD SO MANY LAUGHS AND MEMORIES, NO ONE WILL EVER UNDERSTAND WHAT WE MEANT TO EACH OTHER. YOU WERE THE YING TO MY YANG, THE LIGHT TO MY DARK, THE UMBRELLA FOR MY STORM. I HAVE SO MANY REGRETS. IT WAS SO MANY THINGS LEFT UNSAID, AND THINGS I FELT I COULD HAVE DONE MORE OF. HOWEVER, I DO BELIEVE THAT YOU LEFT THIS PLACE KNOWING WHAT YOU MEANT TO ME AND I CAN REST EASY KNOWING WHAT I MEANT TO YOU. I KNOW YOU ARE UP THERE TELLING THEM DON'T TOUCH YOUR NEW HAIR. ALL THE ANGELS WILL NOW GET TO EXPERIENCE THE HAPPINESS THAT WE DID WITH YOU IN OUR LIFE. I'M SURE YOU'RE UP THERE CRACKING JOKES AND KICKING IT WITH SIDNEY. THAT WAS YOUR HOMEBOY AND NOW YOU ALL ARE REUNITED. I LOVE YOU AND MAKE SURE TO CHECK ON ME FROM TIME TO TIME. I'M GOING TO NEED IT. I LOVE YOU SO MUCH AND I MISS YOU FROM MY SOUL.

ON BEHALF ON BATINA DAVIS, RIP REGGIE GIE-SOUL CRAWFORD. SHE MISSES YOU DEARLY AND I PRAY YOU ARE SLEEPING IN PEACE.

To my daughter. I remember when I sat in front of the doctors when you were three years old and they told me that you were on the spectrum. Immediately, I began to cry. It hurt my heart that it was another battle you had to fight. You had already been through so much, and I couldn't stop the tears from falling. That was until I knew what that meant. I had no idea I was getting a beautiful, very smart, funny, different, and loving child. You have brought me so much joy and I can honestly say you changed me for the better. You are my everything and you will never have to wonder if anyone loves you. I will make sure that you are overflowed with love. You're my heartbeat and I'm blessed to have you. Keep being you and never stop standing out. I LOVE YOU MIRACLE MONÉT RILEY

Acknowledgements

IT'S SO MANY PEOPLE I WANT TO THANK, I OFTEN FORGET. JUST KNOW THAT I LOVE YOU ALL AND I'M GRATEFUL FOR EVERYTHING THAT EVERYONE DOES FOR ME. THE LOVE AND SUPPORT YOU AL GIVE ME IS SIMPLY AMAZING. MY READERS NEVER LET ME DOWN AND I JUST WANT YOU ALL TO KNOW I APPRECIATE YOU FROM THE BOTTOM OF MY HEART.

HAPPY BDAY TO MY SISTER KB COLE, I HOPE YOUR DAY WAS EVERYTHING YOU WANTED AND MORE. YOU'RE SUCH A KIND HEARTED PERSON AND I LOVE YOU FOR ALL THAT YOU ARE AND ALL THAT YOU DO.

HAPPY BDAY TO TONYA MIMS DAUGHTER, SPEND ALL YOUR MOMMY'S MONEY AND I HOPE YOU ENJOYED YOUR DAY BABES.

HAPPY BDAY YOLANDA ANDERSON MAY YOU ENJOY YOUR DAY BABES. THANK YOU FOR YOU CONTINUOUS SUPPORT.

TO MY PUBLISHER, THANK YOU FOR EVERYTHING THAT YOU DO FOR ME. I APPRECIATE ALL OF YOUR SUPPORT AND ALL THE THINGS YOU HAVE INSTILLED IN ME. KEEP BEING YOU AND KEEP PUSHING FORWARD.

TO MY MLPP FAMILY I LOVE YOU GUYS AND OUR TIME IS HERE. DON'T GIVE UP AND ALWAYS AIM HIGH. I LOVE YOU.

TO MY BESTIE, GIRL YOU KNOW I I I LOVE YOU. NO MATTER WHAT YOU DO. LOL THANK YOU BOO FOR BEING THERE FOR ME. I APPRECIATE YOU AND ALL OF OUR TALKS. YOU ARE AMAZING AND I'M GLAD I FOUND SOMEONE LIKE YOU. TELL DONOVAN TWO TO THE FACE IF HE KEEPS PLAYING WITH ME.

TO MY BAE ZATASHA AKA ZEE BAE I'M SO PROUD OF YOU AND ALL THE THINGS YOU ARE ACCOMPLISHING. NEVER LET ANYONE STEAL YOUR DREAMS. THANK YOU FOR ALWAYS BEING THERE FOR ME NO MATTER WHAT. YOU ARE TRULY AMAZING, AND I LOVE YOU.

KRISSY HEY MY OLD BOO. I LOVE YOU AND THANK YOU FOR KEEPING ME ON MY TOES. YOU ARE THE REASON I HAVE TO BE ON POINT. YOU HAVE A GREAT SPIRIT AND I APPRECIATE YOU.
KB COLE I LOVE YOU EVEN THOUGH YOUR ASS BE ACTING FUNNY NOW. YOU ARE MY SISTER FOR LIFE AND I LOVE YOU. KEEP PUSHING OUT THOSE DOPE ASS BOOKS. YOU'RE AN AMAZING PERSON AND I APPRECIATE YOU.

TO MY AMAZING COUSIN, I LOVE YOU SO MUCH AND I DON'T KNOW WHAT I WOULD DO WITHOUT YOUR ASS SOME DAYS. YOU ARE THE SHIT AND I HOPE YOU CHANGE YOUR MIND. YOU ARE A DOPE ASS WRITER, AND EVERYONE NEEDS TO READ

YOUR WORK. IF YOU HAVEN'T CHECKED HER OUT, PLEASE DO SO. AJ DAVIDSON YOU ARE AMAZING DON'T PUT DOWN YOUR PEN.

PANDA I LOVE YOU BOO MAKE SURE YALL GO CHECK OUT HER BOOKS. SHE HAS THE URBAN ROMANCE ON LOCK. KEEP MOVING TOWARDS YOUR GOAL ITS COMING.

BLAKE KARRINGTON THANK YOU FOR EVERYTHING YOU'RE A DOPE AUTHOR AND FRIEND I APPRECIATE YOU YALL GO CHECK OUT HIS CATALOG AND JOIN HIS READING GROUP FOR READERS ONLY.

THANK YOU TO EVERYONE THAT DOWNLOADED THIS BOOK. BEWARE IT IS FILLED WITH DRAMA, LOVE, SEX, AND PETTY LOL I'M GOING IN HIDING ONCE YOU ALL START DOWNLOADING.

SPECIAL THANK YOU TO SHVONNE LATRICE FOR ALLOWING ME TO USE HER AS A CHARACTER VISUAL AND CHARACTER FOR THIS BOOK. I APPRECIATE YOU AND THANK YOU FROM THE BOTTOM OF MY HEART.

WHERE WE LEFT OFF...

SPADE

Sitting in my cell, I couldn't believe my ass was in this shit hole. I've been going over the shit in my mind trying to figure out what the fuck I missed. It had to be Bruno's ass, and I was kicking myself for missing all the signs. That was my lil nigga and I saved Gino from killing him on numerous occasions. This entire time, I thought it was Gino on some snake shit, but it was the lil nigga I raised and groomed from the start.

I've been waiting to hear from Shvonne with some good news that she got a motherfucker to confess, but that shit has yet to happen. It's been six months and we still don't know which one of these niggas set me up. I needed her to torture Bruno and try to get the info out of him. It had to be his ass, that was the only thought I kept coming back to.

This shit was starting to take a toll on me, but it was hitting my mama more. She was looking a fucking mess and every time she came; her ass broke down and left screaming and crying. It got so bad I had to tell her to stay at home. I couldn't stand breaking my moms heart and I was strong enough to do this shit without her having to be here. Shvonne was the ridah I knew she was. My shorty handled all my business and it was good to know I picked the right bitch to be by my side.

"Spade you got a visitor." Knowing it was my shorty, a smile came over my face and for the first time today, my ass was in a good mood. The guard escorted me to the visiting cage and she was sitting there looking like new money. I never had to give her the pass code to my safe because I had too much money coming in. She would be set for the rest of her life just off the work she was putting in. If she ever needed it, I would give to her ass in a heartbeat. The money I got from my father is hidden away. I would never put all my money in one spot and I was glad I did that shit.

"Hey baby. You still looking fine as ever. You better not be somebody's bitch in here. You know I got my ears to the streets and these niggas will come out talking." If she was anybody else, I would have cursed her ass the fuck out for saying some shit like that, but I knew it was her trying to make me smile.

"Get the fuck out of here. You know I go for sentencing tomorrow. It's now or never shorty. I need you to put some pressure on a motherfucker. I'm thinking you need to focus on Bruno. You got to get a nigga to talk or this shit is over for me." You could see the sadness come in her eyes, but she tried not to let it show.

"Your lawyer told me it would be a lost cause. If that was the only thing they had you on, we could work with that. The gun that

8

did the other murders, and the countless bodies they found with the spade on their face is not helping you. I'm so sorry I failed you baby, I really tried to be you." Seeing her cry broke my heart. None of this was on her. It was my dumb ass that thought the shit would be cool if I left my signature on every nigga I killed. It was my ass that got caught with a gun that had bodies on it. My prints were at the scene of the other murder. All that shit fell on me. I hated that she probably sat around blaming herself. I never should have put that kind of pressure on her to make her think my freedom depended on her.

"Look shorty, this shit falls on me. I got too fucking cocky. All I need you to do is stay strong for a nigga. I would never ask you to wait on me, but don't forget about me. Keep my books laced and answer the phone when I call. Is that too much to ask of you?" Shvonne ass started doing the ugly cry and I wish I could hold her. You have enough money to last you a life time, but if you need more I got you. Tell Bruno the business is his. Go live your life shorty."

"I'll come visit every weekend and we don't know how long you are going to get. You can't expect me to just walk away from you. I'll hand everything over to Bruno, but I will not walk away from you." Just knowing she wanted to ride it out with me had a nigga feeling good, but I couldn't ask her to do that shit for me.

"I'll see you tomorrow. Make sure your ass looking good for a nigga. You know you out there representing me and I don't want niggas thinking I had a raggedy bitch."

"You lucky I can't slap your ass. I'll see you tomorrow and I'll pray for you baby." Blowing her a kiss, I got up and walked back to my room. I knew that Bruno confessing wouldn't have gotten me off, but Gino's murder is the one that's getting me connected to the others. The shit at the warehouse could be argued self defense, but none of that mattered without a confession. My fate was in the judge's hands, I just hoped he had mercy on my ass.

****

Shvonne was sitting front row looking good as fuck, smiling at her, I took my seat. The judge walked in and I tried my best to stay looking strong and confident for my shorty, but the shit was hard. My life was in this nigga's hands and I had no idea what he was going to do.

"Jaleel Spade. You are a threat to society and I feel that I would be putting the lives of many in danger if I allow you to walk these streets again. With me knowing the type of pain you have inflicted on thousands of families leads me to believe that you are a terrorist. Therefore, I will sentence you as such. I hereby sentence you to three hundred and twenty five years in prison without the possibility of parole." I never understood why they gave niggas

numbers like that when it wasn't a soul living that long. His bitch ass could have just said life without parole.

All the other shit was just extra. When I heard my shorty scream, it took my mind off of the judge. Turning around to face her, the shit broke my heart. Her body was shaking uncontrollably, and the tears were flowing like a river. Not caring since a nigga wasn't getting out anyway, I reached over the bench and hugged her.

"It's going to be okay shorty. I did this shit to myself. You got enough money to get the fuck out of here. Go live your life. I love you and I'm grateful to have met you." Kissing her, the bailiff started dragging me away. That only made her cry harder. Shit was breaking a nigga.

"I love you shorty, don't you ever forget that."

"I love you to Spade. I'm sorry I never told you, but I love you." When she said that shit, I couldn't stop the tears that fell from my eyes. I could go away knowing I did what I set out to do, I healed her. Now I had to live the rest of my life knowing I broke her again.

****

ONE YEAR LATER...

I've been in Statesville Correctional Facility for a year now and I was just getting to the point where I could go to sleep and not dream about Shvonne. Shorty had me and I couldn't believe I fucked that shit up. Every night, I thought about different shit I could have done to avoid me being here. If I had killed Gino when he first started acting flaw, I never would have taken that meeting and went to kill him after. It was so many mistakes I made and wish I had done shit another way. At the end of the day, all I was doing was torturing myself. The shit was done, and I would die in here. After seeing the toll this shit was taking on Shvonne, I took her off my visitors list and I would only call.

Since I stopped our visits, she sounded like she was doing a lot better. Every time I would call, she would be somewhere else in the world. I wish I could be out there with her enjoying the money I worked so hard for. Instead, the shit was just collecting dust. I've been thinking it over for a while, and I was going to tell her tonight where the rest of the money was with all my pass codes. There was more than enough money on my books and I barely used it. Motherfuckers gave me everything just because I was King Spade.

"Spade nurse visit." I'm glad the finally called me down for it because I had a tooth ache out of this world. When I was heading down the hall, I saw Bruno. If he was in here who the fuck was running the business?

"Nigga what the fuck you doing in here? I know you're not stupid enough to get caught with nothing? If you're here, who the fuck running my shit?" He lucky I even gave it to him since I wasn't sure if he set me up or not.

"Nigga what the fuck are you talking about? The motherfucker you left in charge is running it. Queen P got shit on lock out there." My ass was lost as to who the fuck that was.

"Nigga who the fuck is Queen P?" Now he was looking at me crazy.

"Pebbles nigga. She said you put her in charge and we all been working for her."

"I did put her in charge in the beginning. When I got sentenced, I told her to hand everything over to you."

"She ain't said shit like that to me."

"Spade, let's go." Hurrying my ass to the nurse, I needed to get back to the tier, so I could call her ass. This girl got a taste of the streets and now she was addicted to the shit. My ass done created a monster. With me being in here, I couldn't stop her. If that was the life she wanted to live, then I would let her. She probably feels like it has her closer to me. I wouldn't take that from her, but I was going to curse her ass out about lying to me. If she wanted to stay in charge, I would have let her.

When I got back to the tier, I called her phone, but the number was disconnected. Calling my moms, I had her try to do a three way. I got the same result.

"Ma, go by my house. Something might be wrong. I know you don't like her, but this is not like Shvonne. We talk damn near every day. If somebody set me up, they may have went after her. I'll call you back in an hour."

"Nigga you lucky I love your ass. This Salt Lake butter looking bitch better not give me no attitude either. Your ass chasing her when you got all that boy pussy in there with you."

"Bye ma. I'll call you in an hour." It seemed like time was going by slow as fuck and I was going crazy watching the clock. If something happened to her, I would lose my fucking mind. My ass was pacing the floor and I damn near broke my finger dialing my moms when the hour was up. She answered on the first ring and my heart sank. Someone had done something to my baby. Fuck.

"Son, she cleaned you out. It is nothing in this motherfucker and your safe is wide open and not a rubber band is in that bitch. I told you it was something about her ass, but you didn't want to listen."

"Ma, go to the garage." When she walked in, I could tell my shit was gone. The echo was too damn loud.

"That shit gone too. It is one car in here though. An old ass white Benz with California plates." Hanging up the phone, my heart was racing trying to figure out why Shvonne robbed me. Out of nowhere everything started to hit me at once.

She robbed me when no one in the world was bold enough to do that shit. The first day I met her she was focused on my tattoo. When we were in the car talking, she asked me why did I just up and kill people. Why didn't I need a reason? Every time I turned around, she was crying over her ex that was killed. When I got shot at, I was leaving Shvonne's house. Her best friend leaving with Gino even though she knew what he did to La La and she didn't say a word. Before I left out, I told her I had that meeting and then I was going to Gino's house. In court one of the murders they charged me with was from some guy in California I killed at the club. Shvonne was from California. Her leaving the Benz in my garage was her letting me know.

My ass was standing in the day room having flash back after flash back. Once the shit started running back to me, I knew exactly what the fuck happened. THIS BITCH SET ME UP.

"The court awaited as the foreman got the verdict from the bailiff. Emotional outbursts tears and smeared makeup. He stated, he was guilty on all charges. She's shaking looking like she took it the hardest. A spin artist, she brought her face up laughing. That's when the prosecutor realized what happened. All that speaking her mind testifying and crying when this bitch did the crime. The Queenpin. Before you lock my love away. You need to let me testify." Testify- Common

CHAPTER ONE SPADE

"Spade, you have an attorney visit." Looking up at the guard, I was confused on why my lawyer was coming to see me. Everyone else was in their cells laying down, and I'm being escorted out. Shit had me on alert because attorneys ain't out here doing late night visits. If these niggas thought it would be this easy to take me out, they had another thing coming.

I've been locked up for almost three years now. It's been a year and a half since I realized the bitch I was in love with was setting me up from the start. I've tried my best to replay that night in California in my mind, but the shit was a blur. I remember killing dude for popping off about his bitch, but for the life of me I couldn't figure out how Shvonne knew it was me. Me and her didn't have any type of interaction, and I don't remember telling them where I was from.

I had the slightest idea how she found me, but I do know the shit was intentional. My ass would have preferred her ass to try and take me out or let me know we were at war. The way she did that shit was straight savage, and I had to give it up to her for that shit. If Shvonne had done it any other way, she would have lost. Her and that nigga from LA would have had one hell of a reunion. This bitch was calculated though.

Her confidence is what got me the most. When she robbed me, she knew that would draw me out. The fact that she assumed I would try to fuck and not kill her let me know she was a different kind of crazy. That nigga had her mind twisted and I wish I could help them reunite. Every time I thought about the shit, I would get three fifty hot. This bitch was sure of herself, she took my own money and put it on my books. Shvonne kept my shit laced. How the fuck savage was that? Like nigga I know that you done found out I took your shit, but I'm going to be generous enough to make sure your ass not in there struggling.

All this time, I thought Gino and Bruno were the snake ass niggas, when Pebbles was behind everything. The more I thought about that shit, the more I laughed. Even though I killed every motherfucker they charged me with except Gino, I couldn't believe that bitch got me over three hundred years in this bitch. When I made it into the visiting room, it was a fine ass woman standing there. Looking back at the guard, I tried to make sure this was the right room. This damn sure wasn't my attorney and it's been too long since I got some pussy. My dick was brick hard and she smirked as if she could tell.

"Jaleel Spade it's nice to meet you. I'm State's Attorney Valencia Brolen. Officer, can you excuse us for a minute?" Even though she was fine as hell, I had nothing to say to this bitch. When

I tried to tell them I didn't have shit to do with Gino's death, they ass ain't have shit to say.

"You don't have to leave. Take me back to my room. Y'all got me fucked up if y'all think I'm about to sit in here and talk to this bitch. They gave me my time, and I accepted the shit." Her face expression changed, and the bitch went the fuck off.

"JALEEL SIT THE FUCK DOWN. YOUR ASS GOT THREE HUNDRED YEARS, I'M SURE YOU HAVE TIME TO SPARE FIVE MINUTES. When I'm done, if you still want to leave then by all means you can get the fuck out, but you will listen to what I have to say." Me and the guard both laughed. She thought her antics moved me. I sat down because I was curious to know what the fuck she had to say to me.

"Don't get shit twisted. I'm still King Spade in this bitch and if you ever talk to me like that again, they gone be adding some more time to my shit. Now, if you have something to say, say it. Check your tone though." She waited until the officer closed the door and started to speak.

"A week ago, I just buried my son. It was my only child and I refuse to accept his death. No matter how hard I tried to give him a good life, he still got caught up in the street life." Looking at her uninterested, I was trying to figure out what the fuck this shit had to do with me. Nothing about this was my concern, and I was ready to go back to my cell.

"You're wasting my time. I don't see why the fuck you're here talking to me about your son. I'm tired, and I would really like to go back to my cell." She looked irritated, but not more than me.

"To make a long story short, he ended up owing some bad people some money. They didn't realize they were putting all these drugs and trust into the hands of a drug user. They killed him, and I want revenge." Hearing her say that piqued my interest, but I was still lost on why she was here. My ass was going to be in here for over three hundred years.

"Okay." The bitch had the nerve to smack her lips. She was acting as if she gave me enough clues to figure out what the fuck she was talking about.

"Okay, those bad people are the same bad people that set your ass up." Now that had my attention. "He worked for Queen P aka Shvonne Lavigne. I've tried everything to take that bitch down, but she is too smart. As a mother, I can't let that shit go. I need her to pay for what she did to my son. After going over everything and piecing shit together, I realized that you may have been set up by your own girl. I'm sure you want to get some kind of revenge. So, I'm proposing a truce. I'll write up some kind of technicality to get you out of here, but you have to handle that one thing for me." Not sure if she was serious or not, I didn't know how to respond.

"What guarantees will I have that you won't try to put me back in here once I'm done with what you need?"

"Once you are released, the state can't lock you back up. They would have to take you back to trial and it would have to be on a different charge. As long as you don't do anything to get caught on a new charge, you're a free man. If your dumb ass go out there and do some dumb shit, you deserve to be back in here."

"And killing somebody for the State's Attorney ain't dumb? You want me to trust a motherfucker that got me locked the fuck up. I don't trust you and you don't trust me. How the fuck is that going to work?"

"To show you that I trust you and to make you more comfortable with me, I'm going to let you stay at my place until the shit is complete. That way, you know my every move and I know yours. I could lose my job if anyone found out you were at my house, and I'm willing to risk it. I'll also be able to watch you and make sure you're doing what you are supposed to be doing." Of course, I didn't want to live in this bitch shit, but it would make me feel secure in her position.

"If I do this, just know it's on my own terms and time. You don't dictate shit I do and you're not my boss. You sit behind a desk in a skirt. I'm not jeopardizing my life or freedom and you know nothing about that street life shit. Let me do me and we have a deal."

"As long as you don't try to play me, we are good. Give me a few days and everything will be in play. I won't be back here, they will release you and leave as if you would have gotten out. I'll meet you at your house. "

"How the fuck am I supposed to get there?"

"Either call somebody to come get you, or get your ass on that Greyhound. Either way, I'll meet you at your address. We can't be seen together after this. See you in a few days." Walking back to my cell with the guard, I couldn't wipe the smile off my face. Pebbles was in for a rude awakening and that bitch wouldn't know what hit her. She thought she got rid of me, but King Spade was back, and that bitch was about to feel my wrath.

The excitement was brewing, and I couldn't sleep. Pulling out this book one of the homies gave me, I started reading *When Love Calls Your Name by AJ Davidson.* It was a novella and didn't take long to read. I'm a street nigga and that shit had my ass tearing up. Looking for some hardcore shit, I decided to read *She Gave Her Heart to The Realest by Yanni.* This was better for a nigga like me. Especially since I had revenge on my mind. I was trying to figure out how I could love and hate a person at the same time. I couldn't wait to see Pebbles, but I'm sure I was the last person she wanted or expected to see.

CHAPTER TWO SHVONNE

Sitting here with my Chanel heels kicked up on my desk, I felt on top of the world. I was able to accomplish something none of these niggas were able to do. Single handedly, I took down King Spade and he never saw it coming. From the moment he killed Bam at the club, I knew I was going after that nigga. It wasn't until I was laid up in the hospital, I remembered Bam asking him where he was from and he told him Chicago. Once he left his signature mark on his cheek, I knew he wouldn't be hard to find. It was like following a paper trail.

There was no way it was two niggas in Chicago carving spades in people faces. When I moved to Chicago, I couldn't find him directly. Knowing I would have to draw him out, I assembled a team of bitches that would help me rob them blind. None of them knew what I had planned, so they were involved but without knowing they were. Following them, I saw Gino beating the shit out of La La and I knew she was our way in. Even though most people would assume Gino was in on it, he wasn't. His ass had no idea his bitch was robbing him for his own money. The shit was brilliant if I do say so myself. A bitch played the fuck out of her part, but I didn't plan on falling for him. No matter what I felt, I had to avenge Bam and my child he killed. Everything I did was calculated, even bringing Tiana here. I needed her to fuck around with Gino so that we could get him alone to kill his ass. Seeing Spade left his knife, that was the perfect set up.

Knowing he would call and see that my number and shit was changed, I knew he would send someone to his house. A bitch cleaned that nigga out and went and bought a Benz just like the one that Bam gave me. Putting Cali plates on it was the finishing touch, leaving that as the only clue, I knew he would put the shit together. I thought I would feel good about the shit, but I didn't. My ass still wondered if I did the right thing every day.

Spade tried to heal me, but I fought him at every turn. How could I love the nigga that took my true love away from me? Would Bam forgive me for that shit? Or would I always feel like the traitor I knew I would have been? That shit was a hard decision to make. Scared to love someone again, I chose to go with what I knew. Spade could hurt me or leave me. I didn't know how our story would have ended, but I knew Bam. Looking at Spade was a constant reminder of the hurt he caused me. His ass tried to give me his all, but I didn't want it. All I could see was revenge and I ignored the feelings in my heart for him.

For the longest, the necklace around my neck reminded me of Spade every day. When I would feel tears fighting their way up, or out of nowhere sadness would take over me. I knew I loved him, but none of that mattered. To this day, I wore the chain he gave me. Whenever I had to make big decisions or something difficult came along, I would rub the spade. It made me feel closer to him and I could try to figure out how Spade would handle the situation. Looking at the door, I now had something different to remind me of Spade every day.

"Mommy nap." Tiana and my daughter Jalayia walked in. I nick named her Jelly because it was easier for her to learn. Since Tiana wasn't really about the street life, she helped me out with my daughter a lot. When Spade stopped me from coming to visit him, I was six months pregnant. My ass did a great job of hiding it with pretty ass flared shirts. When I had her, I started visiting him in the penitentiary. I wanted to tell him, but I knew if I did, my guilt would take over. Keeping his daughter from him was harder than I thought it would be. Jelly was almost two and she was smart as hell. Everything about her reminded me of him. She was his twin and I never seen a girl that small with so much confidence.

"Come here and give mama a hug. I missed you, did you miss me?"

"Jelly miss mommy." Laughing, I picked her up and planted kisses all over her face. Sitting her down in my chair, I gave her some crayons and paper. I could tell Tiana wanted to talk to me, so I pulled her to the side.

"I ran into Ms. Janice today at Walmart. She was talking to Jelly and I snatched her and got the fuck out of there." Me and Tiana saw her a couple of weeks ago, luckily she didn't see me. I snatched Tiana and damn near ran the sole off my shoes. It wasn't that I was scared of her, I would beat that bitch to sleep. I didn't know who she had with her or if they would follow me. Spade never talked about having family, but I wanted to make sure I was careful. His mama was with King Leel for years, she had to pick up some kind of street smarts. I would never underestimate anyone like Spade did me.

"She doesn't know who either of you are, but it was good you got the fuck up out of there. They say mamas be knowing their grandkids and shit. Even if me and Spade was good, I wouldn't want that bitch around my baby. The bitch rude as hell."

"Umm you are too. That is the only family she has left. You don't think it's fucked up that she don't know she has a grandchild?" Looking at her like she was crazy, I almost cursed her ass out. I've been working on not spazzing out so easy lately.

"No harder than keeping her from her father. Fuck her. Me and Spade made that baby, not me and his loose tooth ass mama. Me and that bitch don't get along and refuse to have her around my child. Get off that mother Theresa shit and be her auntie. She got us and that's enough. When she gets older, if she feels she want to sit in a waiting room every weekend for three hundred years, that's on her."

"Bitch you foul as fuck for that shit. You're her mom, so I'm going to leave it alone. All I'm saying is you stripped him of

25

everything and you took her son away from her, letting her see the baby wouldn't hurt nobody." This bitch had to be sniffing some of my product or her meds was getting the best of her. Either way, the bitch was losing it.

"Tiana, do you hear yourself? That bitch might try to take my baby or kill me to have her. She was a street bitch, I don't trust that hoe.

"Okay." Not wanting to be bothered with her any longer, I grabbed Jelly and headed home.

"Tell the fellas to call me if something happens. I'm out." Jumping in my Maserati, I headed to my mansion I had built. There was no way I would stay in Spade's house. It wasn't that I was mad at Tiana, I just didn't like talking about that shit. In due time I would have a lot of questions to answer, right now, I just wanted to enjoy my child.

Nothing about that situation sounded like some shit I wanted to do. I had no verifiable income, and Ms. Janice petty ass might try to take her from me. That old bitch was mean as fuck and probably be over there fucking my baby up just because she was half mine. Spade was gone, and I wasn't about to rock the boat if I didn't have to. She had me and that was all she needed.

CHAPTER THREE VALENCIA

"I'm not going to his grave with you Valencia. All this shit is your fault. I should have stepped in a long time ago. You were always so hard on Shawn and I allowed you to do it. Now you want to cry and act like we were a big happy family."

"Franklin how the fuck was it my fault? All I wanted was what was best for him. Pushing him to do better in school or hanging with the right people was being too hard on him? What was I supposed to do? Let him do what the fuck he wanted or should I have let him run around fucking everything moving like you."

"Don't put that shit on me. Who I fucked had no bearings on me being a father."

"It does when you're never there. You would rather lay up with some bitch than to be at home with your own family. We needed you and I was left to pick up the pieces. Don't you dare try to make this out to be my fault."

"Fuck you Valencia. You can go put flowers on a grave or do whatever else it is that you think will help you feel better. We both know your overbearing ass is the reason he turned to drugs." When the phone hung up, I was livid. My husband, soon to be ex was always blaming me. Anything that went wrong, it was my fault. I couldn't do anything right in his eyes. Not even fuck, which is why he was sleeping with anything with a pussy and legs.

Yes, I pushed my son. All I was trying to do was make him better. Drugs was his choice because of the crowd he hung in. Nothing I could have done or said would have prevented that. To me, Franklin was talking out of his ass. How does he know what I did wrong when he was never here? The nigga didn't even come home to say he was leaving. His ass just never came back for his belongings.

Even when Shawn died, he did nothing to try and figure out what went wrong. My ass got out there in the streets doing footwork to find out what the fuck happened. It was me that found out who he was working for and who killed him. I took everything I had to my supervisor, but they told me I had a bunch of circumstantial evidence. None of the evidence was enough for me to bring Queen P in. My ass stalked and followed her for months and I knew the information I found out was true. It was no way for me to get the stuff I needed, but I could still take her ass down.

She was a low life street bitch and I knew I would have to deal with her as such. Thinking of everything under the sun, Jaleel finally popped in my head. His attorney kept saying he was being set up. After going back over his case with a fine tooth comb, I knew he didn't kill Gino. The spade was even carved differently.

With all the other murders he had done, my coworker wasn't trying to hear nothing about him being set up.

After doing some digging, I pieced together that Jaleel killed her boyfriend in California. The shit was brilliant, but she wasn't as slick as she thought.

You going down you gutta rat bitch.

When I'm upset, I tend to talk to myself a lot. Lately, that's all I been doing. Knowing Jaleel wouldn't be able to resist my offer, I went to see him. His ass was still cocky for a nigga that wasn't going to see the time of day. What he didn't know was, my ass was from the hood too. Yes, I needed him, but nobody was going to talk to me like I was beneath them. He was going to hear what I had to say, whether he wanted to or not.

After he agreed, the adrenaline was running through my veins like hot blood. I could almost taste the revenge. When I got into my profession, I did it to make sure that everyone had a fair shot. To see justice served and it would be fair. I was young and ambitious. My people always said they didn't get a fair shake, and I was there to make sure that happened. I never expected it to fail me. Where was the system when my son needed them?

Grabbing my flowers, I headed to my son's gravesite. My husband could never agree on anything, but I thought he would at least be here for me with this. Getting out of the car, each step I took broke me down. No mother should ever have to bury their child, but I did.

"Hey son. I know you think we forgot about you, but I've been working hard to bring you justice. I know that you were a good child that got caught up with the wrong crowd. Just know that I'm not mad at you. It hurts every day just thinking about you and our memories. People say that memories supposed to make you feel better, but that's not the case. The shit hurts, and it hurts bad.

Nobody ever prepares you for a pain like this. There are no kind words or grand gestures that heals a mother's broken heart. Shawn, I tried to protect you. Why wouldn't you listen? Why did you fight me at every corner? Now I have to fight myself to sleep at night. My heart is empty, but I won't rest until someone else is feeling the same way I do. I love you baby."

The last thing I ever thought I'd do was break the law, but a mother's love outweighed any sane thought we may have. There was no way that bitch would walk these streets and my son was buried in some damn dirt. I want her to suffer how I think my son did. Jaleel was perfect for that job.

Jumping in my car, I headed to his house to meet him there. It would be hard having him living with me, especially since he is the finest man I ever laid eyes on. Everything about him screamed bitch you are going to get sprung. Luckily, what we had going on was business. I wasn't trying to fuck with Spade, I needed him to avenge my son.

If he tried to fuck me over, by the time I'm done with him, he would wish he had just killed the bitch. Nothing is going to stop me from getting justice, not even Jaleel Spade. I was going to get him home with some techs on the police, but he better keep his fucking word, or it will be hell to pay.

CHAPTER FOUR SPADE

As soon as the fresh air hit my face, a nigga could have cried. You never appreciate your freedom until the shit is taken from you. I thought I was untouchable and that bitch Shvonne knocked me off my high horse. It was something I never saw coming. The entire time I was watching Gino, when it was her I should have kept my eye on. Everything she took from me, I could get back. Everything except my heart. That bitch had a hold on me, and I didn't know how to release that shit. I still dream about her ass, but no matter how I feel, I had to get my revenge.

She crossed the line, but I was about to drop kick her ass right on back over. She did all this shit over a nigga with a big mouth, now, she was going to be able to live in peace with his ass. My ego told me there was no way I could let that shit ride, but my heart was telling me it was no way I could kill her. Knowing my freedom depended on it, her ass was about to be goat meat.

"What the fuck you doing? Thinking about how much booty you're about to be missing? Get your ass in the car, I promise it's plenty of niggas that is willing to give it up. Over there daydreaming and shit. Bring your ass on." My mama was standing there with her arms opened wide smiling like a nigga watching kids at the park. She couldn't be normal and just tell me how much she missed me.

Instead, she had to show her ass out here like I was a bitch ass nigga.

"Ma, I haven't been out five minutes. Don't start that shit. Let me at least get in the car." Walking towards her, I gave her the biggest hug I could muster up.

"That's what I said. You yellow niggas sholl be sensitive." We climbed in the car and she hugged me again. Even though there were tears in her eyes, her words would never match her emotions. "Do you trust this lady that got you out? What do you have to do? Where are you going to stay?" Her ass was firing off question after question.

"I don't know if I could trust her, but so far she has kept her word. It's not like she can put me back in there or her ass will get in trouble. She has a vendetta with Pebbles and wants me to handle it. To make sure neither one of us cross each other, I'm going to live with her." My mama head whipped around so fast, her wig shifted.

"We don't know this lady. Why the fuck do you have to live with her? I just got your ass back. You trying to go back to your boyfriend or something ain't you?"

"Ma, can you stop. It's part of the deal and I'll be straight. We have a common enemy and trust me, nobody can play my ass again."

"If your beady eye ass had listened to me, you wouldn't be in this predicament. I knew that girl wasn't shit. You can't trust a black girl with that much hair. Hoe knows voodoo or something. Even though I don't like her ass, I don't agree with you doing somebody else's dirty work. You get your hands dirty and her ass clear and free. We don't move like that son. Everybody gotta put in their own work. You can make the meet up happen but let her do her own shit." She may have thought I wasn't listening, but I wouldn't make that mistake again. She was right. If I got caught, or she set me up my ass was back in jail. Meanwhile, she would be free and clear. She knows a nigga like me would never snitch.

"I hear you ma."

"I hope so, I heard niggas around here nutting in people's ears and shit. Who in the fuck would think of some nasty ass shit like that?"

"We are not about to have this conversation. Hurry up and get me home, so I can meet this lady before her ass thinks I'm not coming and send the police after my ass."

"The bitch can try it. Put your seatbelt on." Doing as I was told, I laughed as I closed my eyes. It was pros and cons to having parents from the streets. My mama could read people and my dumb ass didn't listen. I was blinded by the pussy lips, but she felt it. The negative side to that shit is, they always thought they knew everything. She talked shit and I had to take it. I had a lot of time to think about how I wanted to play this shit on the way to my house. It didn't sit right with me that a motherfucker wanted me out there

34

getting caught up in some more shit. She also said if I lived with her, she could watch my every move. I had to make sure her ass had no ties to me and I could move freely. Whatever I did, it would be because I felt that shit. If my gut was telling me to leave it alone, then that's what I would do. I learned a hard lesson and I would never allow my ego to get in the way of my thinking again.

Finally pulling up to the house, I saw she was waiting outside of the gate. Not wanting her inside of my shit, I had my mama park on the side of her. We both got out and she just stared at me. The shit kind of made me feel uncomfortable, and I knew I had to watch her sneaky ass.

"Are you going to grab some stuff? We can ride together and get you settled in. On tomorrow we will go over the game plan." She was barking orders as if I didn't tell her this was my show.

"What did I tell you? I'm going to do this my way, on my time. If you can't deal with that, we can cut ties now. It's nothing in there. You can give me your address and I'll meet you there later. I need to drop her off and pick some things up. I'll be there in a few hours." You could tell she wanted to protest, but she knew it wouldn't be in her best interest.

"Don't try to play me Jaleel. I got you a phone, I'll text you the address and you have a few hours or..." Stepping close to her face, I let her know her threats didn't mean shit.

"Or what? Remember that you need me. I no longer need you. Don't forget that."

"That's right tell that bitch son. For what it's worth, I don't trust her fake ass either. She looking at you like you're beneath her. Let mama know if you need me to knock her ass down a notch or two. Stiff ass bitch standing there with her nose turned up. I bet she aint know she got a booger in her nose." My mama done rolled down the window and got all in our business. I found the shit funny, of course Valencia didn't. You could see the steam coming off her ass. The funny part was, she wanted to dig in her nose so bad to see if it really was a booger, but she was too stuck up to do the shit. Her ass didn't have to go far because it was hanging out and shit. Jumping back in the car with my mama, I rolled the window up without even looking her way. A few seconds later, an address came through and I put the phone up.

When we got to my mama's house, I didn't even go in. I climbed in the driver side and pulled off. My mama knew I was on my way to Pebbles, she knew her son. I wasn't going to make a move, but I wanted to see her. I had to see her.

When I pulled up to the warehouse, she was walking out. I was pissed at myself when my dick jumped. She looked sexy as hell. Wearing a two piece suit and heels, Pebbles actually looked like a bitch in charge. She wore no bra, but her breast sat up perfectly in the jacket. Pebbles was walking in her heels with authority. Not even looking around, she got in her car and drove off. That told me she was running the fuck out of my city. In her mind, niggas feared her too much to try her. I missed that feeling, I knew that shit all too well.

I followed her with ease, she had no idea I was behind her. It helped that no one but my moms knew I was out. We finally pulled up to a big ass mansion. I think she tried to outdo my shit. The only thing she was missing was the gate that you needed a passcode to get in. I watched her get out and a little girl and Tiana came walking out. The little girl ran to her and Pebbles picked her up swinging her around.

When the fuck did she have a baby? When she was visiting me, she wasn't pregnant, so it had to be somebody else's child. That shit really broke my heart because I tried like hell to get her ass pregnant. Now this bitch was laid up living the life with the next nigga. That shit struck a nerve in me and I drove off with murder on my mind. I would be back to pay Pebbles a visit. For now, I was going to let her make it.

Not even worrying about clothes and money right now, it was only one thing I wanted. Heading to my safe house that no one knew about, I put the code in and grabbed a few guns. I needed my rifle in order to do what I needed from a distance. Making sure I had ammo, I headed back to Pebble's house. Parking a block away, I made my way into one of her neighbor's yard. Using the tree, I climbed on top of their roof and waited for my moment.

She wanted to play games, but I was the master of those. I was going to do her how she did me, but worse. Her and this bitch ass friend of hers fucked with the wrong crew. Licking my lips, I smiled as the war began.

CHAPTER FIVE SHVONNE

"Mommy." Seeing my daughter run to my arms every time she saw me made me feel like I was on top of the world. No amount of power could match that feeling.

"Hey Jelly. Were you a good girl for auntie Tiana?"

"Yes." I laughed as she nodded her head fast as hell. Carrying her in the house, I took her upstairs to her room. I had a date tonight, but I wanted to be the one to bathe her and put her down for bed. Tiana didn't mind watching her since she really had no life. The only time she really came out is if I made her go to the club with me or if I needed her to handle some business. It's like she had become depressed as hell out of nowhere.

"You didn't take your clothes off, where your ass going?" Tiana was smiling at me like she knew I had a date.

"Me and Hanz going out tonight. I'm finally about to give his ass the goodies." Walking out of the bathroom, I stood in the hallway to have this conversation. I didn't want Jelly to hear me, but I wanted to be close enough to make sure she was good. Tiana followed behind me and I continued.

"Girl this pussy ain't been touched since the doctors pulled Jelly out. I need some dick. I'm tired of using Feelo. I need to feel the real thing. I saw his ass in some jogging pants today and a bitch couldn't stop watching that thing flap in the wind."

39

"Make sure you strap up and fuck his ass like your coochie's lifespan depends on it." Laughing, I walked back in the bathroom to wash up Jelly. Whenever she talked like that, I never knew what to say. It was like walking on egg shells if you mentioned condoms and safe sex. Her ass was depressed enough. Besides, Jelly was all I needed. Once I was done, I put her in the bed and read her a story. As soon as her eyes closed for five seconds, I knew she was out. Getting up, I grabbed my phone and texted Hanz my address.

Jumping in the shower, I freshened up since I knew I was about to give him all this pussy. Once I was done, I threw on a Pink jogging suit and some Jordans. Hanz was a hood nigga and he wouldn't care if I dressed down. Tiana called my name and I knew that he was there. Grabbing my purse, I headed out the door. Licking his lips, he grabbed me to him and cuffed my ass. Out of nowhere, something wet splattered all over my face. Feeling Hanz's body go limp, I pulled away and saw the blood pouring from his head. Pushing him off me, I looked around trying to figure out who the fuck shot him. When I didn't see anybody, I grabbed my phone.

"Hey Tay, I need you to bring the clean up crew to my house. I'll text you the address. They need to get here right fucking now. When you're done, everybody needs to meet me at the warehouse. I'll be there waiting." Hanging up the phone, I went in the house to let Tiana know what was going on.

"Somebody just killed Hanz right on our fucking door step. I have to go out, but I'll be back. The crew will be here shortly. Let them in." Not waiting on a response, I went back to my room and jumped my ass back in the shower. On the outside, I looked calm as hell, but on the inside, I was shaking.

****

Walking back and forth in front of my crew, I swung my bat around for emphasis. Someone in here knew what the fuck happened, and I wanted answers. Everyone looked at me with fear in their eyes, but I had to stay strong. If I showed any sign of weakness, they would take advantage of that shit. It was only two people out of my crew who knew where I lived. The only reason Lil Keith did was because I needed him to pick up some work from me. I knew Jelly and Tiana was at a doctor's appointment.

Walking in front of Lil Keith, I swung my bat like I had to hit that shit out of the park. His forehead caved in, and his body fell limp. Making sure he was gone, I hit his ass again. His body began to shake and then it stopped. I knew he was gone. Walking over to Tay, I hit his ass over the head. That nigga wouldn't fall, and it took me about ten hits to kill that nigga. I knew he wasn't the one that shot Hanz, but I wasn't going to allow someone else to know where

I lived. I wish I knew what niggas he took to clean that shit up and they ass would be dead too. Looking at the men that were left standing there, I pointed my bat at them.

"Does anyone else in here know where I live?" They all screamed no together and I headed out of the warehouse. Looking back, I threw out one last demand.

"I fucked up my Space Jam Jordans. You Motherfuckers got three days to find me another pair. Clean this shit up." Walking out, I got in my car and threw up. I couldn't believe somebody tried to kill me tonight. Was this shit my karma? Hoping I got to the bottom of this shit by killing the people that knew where I lived, I drove home to Jelly. I couldn't allow anyone to harm her because of my shit. I would die trying to protect her, but I would rather kill the bitch ass nigga that was trying.

As soon as I got home, I ran upstairs and jumped my ass in the shower for the third time in two hours putting on a gown, I went to Jelly's room and climbed in the bed with her. She was so innocent, and it killed me to think someone would try to harm her over some shit I did. I knew Tiana would try and lecture me in the morning, but I wasn't trying to hear that shit. She wanted me to walk away from the life, but the power had me gone in the head. I needed that shit and I wasn't giving it up. If a motherfucker wanted a war, they would get one.

Waking up, Jelly was staring me in my face looking like she was trying to figure out why I was in her bed. Laughing, I pulled her to me and started kissing her all over the face.

"Why are you woke so early?"

"Pannicakes." Knowing it wasn't any food in the house, I got up and went to my room and threw on some clothes. Doing the same for her, I grabbed my purse to take her to IHOP. As soon as I opened the door, I screamed. Looking around, I didn't see anybody there.

"Baby go in the house with auntie Tiana. I'll be in there in a few minutes."

"Pannicakes."

"I know baby, we will go in a few minutes." Once she was all the way inside, I walked around my house to see if anyone was still out there. Someone had left Hanz's hand on my porch. The only reason I knew it was his was because of his ring. If the clean up crew got rid of the body, how in the fuck did his hand end up on my porch? Walking in the house, I went to get a garbage bag so I could dispose of the shit. My hands were shaking so bad, I could barely pull it apart. Scooping that shit up, I walked it to the garbage can in my driveway.

Running my ass back in the house, I went to the fridge to get some water. My ass felt like I was about to pass out and I needed a drink. Nothing could have prepared me for the shit I was about to see when I pulled that bitch open. Hanz's head was sitting right there looking at me. No matter how strong I pretended to be, I couldn't fake that shit no more. I screamed and passed the fuck out.

CHAPTER SIX HALLE

Everybody always looked as me as the bitch in Pebbles shadow, but I wasn't. She was going through something and I felt bad for her. That was the only reason I let her get away with so much. There was nothing weak about me, but my edges and I'm working on them bitches. Jamaican Castor Oil was going to get me together though.

Spade got locked up and that bitch changed. Everything was all about her as if the Take Money Crew didn't have her back the entire time. We been living together since she been here, now the bitch treat us like the help. Not needing that kind of stress in my life, I told her ass she could kick rocks. Bitch didn't even blink an eye when I said the shit. It was right around the time she was going into labor.

"Now that I'm in charge, this is how the shit gone go. Bruno is going to be my right hand, Tiana is going to be my left. If I'm available, you need to go down the chain of command. No one is to hit my line directly. All calls go through Bruno first. If I'm here at the warehouse, I'll talk to you in the order of importance. Don't waste my time, if you know the shit ain't important don't bring it to me." Me and Norie started laughing. *"Did I miss something? What the fuck is funny?"* Norie looked at me, and we tried to figure out if she was playing or not.

"Girl bye. Your ass in here acting like the God father and shit. Besides, how the fuck them niggas over us? We were the ones that was here from the jump." Norie was pissed, but I knew Pebbles was about to pop off on her ass.

"I don't give a fuck if you wiped my ass when I was shitting. This is how the shit is going to go. If anybody has a problem with it, they can get the fuck out." Looking over at Norie, that was my cue. She had me fucked up if she thought I was going to kiss her ass.

"Guess it was nice knowing your ass. Y'all can have this shit. Norie you coming?" When she didn't move, I knew her weak ass was going to stay. Shaking my head, I walked out the door. I kind of expected her ass to come behind me, we had been through a lot and she was treating us like a bitch that had to audition for Simon Cowell. Pants on the ground looking ass bitch. Jumping in my car, I drove to the condo. I didn't need that bitch and obviously, she didn't need me.

I've been rocking on my own since. Even though Bruno was still working for her, we kept fucking around. It didn't take long before he took the fall for her shit. Nobody in the crew ever went to jail when they were working for Spade. That just showed me she really didn't know what she was doing. My nigga got bumped on a run. Finally, he was on his way home and I was getting dressed to go pick him up. Making sure I looked sexy for his ass, I jumped in my car and drove the long ass drive to the prison.

As soon as he came out of the door, I jumped out of the car and ran towards him. He picked up some weight and it looked good as fuck on him. His dick rose beneath me, and I couldn't wait to get home and show him what the fuck he missed out on.

"What up shorty? You looking good as fuck." Smiling, I switched my ass back to the car.

"And you looking all daddyish. Now get the fuck in the car so we can go home. You about to be eating a lot of pussy. Hope them lips aint got stretched out in that motherfucker."

"Don't get your dumb ass knocked out. Speaking of bitches." I looked at him and laughed. We were not speaking on bitches, but he said that shit like that's what we were discussing. "What's up with your girl?" Not sure why he was asking about Pebbles, I side eyed the fuck out his ass.

"Fuck you asking about her for?"

"When I got locked up, I saw Spade. Nigga told me that he gave me keys to the streets. That bitch told me he put her in charge. She got me out here working for her, taking risks, and getting my ass locked up when I'm the one supposed to be in charge. Shorty got shit fucked up." That shit only made me hate her more.

"That raggedy ass bitch. I don't fuck with her, but she the type that always get what's coming to her. What you want to do?"

"Swing me by the warehouse. I'm about to take what's mine. Shorty gone bow down or get knocked down. The man said out of his own mouth the shit was mine." Driving fast as hell, I took us to the warehouse. I couldn't wait to see the look on her face. As soon as we pulled up, Bruno jumped out of the car. The shit had barely stopped, and his ass was power walking towards the door. Following behind him, I smiled on my way in. First Lady sounds good to me, and I couldn't wait.

"What's up Pebbles? I see you holding my shit down. Good looking. Give me all the info you got and set up a meeting with a connect." My pussy got wet just watching him take charge.

"I heard they smuggle drugs in jail. I'm guessing your ass done had some ass coke. Shit done fucked your mind up. You can't be smoking drugs out of ass cracks. You don't know what they been eating my nigga." This bitch Pebbles was so cocky, I hated her ass.

"Bitch you think this shit a joke? I talked to Spade when I was in there and he told me that he handed over everything to me. You think you about to sit up in here comfortable, and I watch you run my shit? Bitch I will kill your hoe ass." Everyone in the warehouse was staring on in disbelief. Pebbles laughed and stood up. Raising her arms, I thought the hoe was about to pull a Phantom. Instead, her entire crew stood up off that command and drew their guns.

"Come take it." Bruno had no win and she knew that. Once she realized his ass was about to cower out, she continued to talk shit. "I've always liked you Bruno, but you just pissed me off. I'm going to show you what happens when you bite the hand that feeds you. If anybody even serve this nigga a milk shake, you're dead. If you see this nigga buying a cigarette, shoot his ass. If this nigga drive down the street and look at the warehouse, deaden his ass. Are we clear?"

Everybody nodded their head in agreement. One of her lil niggas walked up on us with his gun. I guess that was our cue to get the fuck out. Not wanting to die today, I did a David Ruffin spin and got the fuck up out of there. When I got in the car and heard Bruno's door open, I knew he did the same thing. You could tell he was pissed, but it was nothing we could do. That bitch had that shit on lock and she knew it. Karma was a bitch though and I hope she hit that hoe over the head. Pebbles thought she was so fucking smart, but one thing you can't do is out smart karma.

"You okay baby?" That nigga looked at me with death in his eyes.

"What the fuck you think? Shut the fuck up and drive." Nigga wanna get tough with me, but he ain't say shit back to Pebbles ass. Everybody wanted to treat me like I wasn't shit, but I was gone show his ass. Tonight, he was getting some of that Suge Avery lemonade. I was gone piss all in his shit.

49

CHAPTER SEVEN VALENCIA

Driving as fast as I could, I tried my best to beat Jaleel to my house. If he thought for one second I was going to trust his ass that easily, he had me fucked up. I knew he was about to run back to that bitch, and I needed to make sure he was still on board. Seeing him watch that bitch pissed me off. You could tell he was still obsessed with her.

When he drove off to some house, he came out with a bunch of guns. I knew he was pissed and I got excited as hell. Anticipation was killing me waiting for him to go kill that bitch. I followed him back to her house and waited for him to do what he did best. Seeing a nigga pull up, I knew that would give him the fire that he needed to shoot her. Since I was in my car and nobody could see me, I did the Stevie J hand rub. My ass even turned my face up like he does. In public, I had to act classy so I would never do that shit if someone was watching me.

Imagine my disappointment and shock, when he shot the guy that came over instead of Pebbles. The one thing I prayed wasn't true, just became obvious. He still loved her. Knowing what was at stake, I had to pull some tricks out the bag. He needed to stay focused and I would need to figure out a way to do that.

First, I had to get the fuck home before he got his ass there. If he knew I was out following him, that nigga would go the fuck off.

Even though I put on a good front back at the jail, he scared the shit out of me. It was something menacing about him and you could tell he wasn't to be fucked with. Pulling on my block, I sighed from relief until I saw his mama's car parked in my driveway. How the fuck did this nigga beat me here? Thinking of a lie, I walked towards the door.

"What the fuck did I tell you?" Damn near jumping out of my skin, I turned around to face him. I don't know where that nigga came from, but he snuck up on me quick as hell.

"What the hell is wrong with you? I can't leave my own house. I went to handle some business. It's good to know you follow instructions well. I would hate to think you trying to play me." As soon as I looked in his eyes, I could see where I had him fucked up at. That nigga didn't believe a word I said. Grabbing me by my neck, he slammed me on the hood of his car. "Please, let me go." It was just above a whisper since he was choking the wind beneath my wings.

"Stop fucking following me. I told you I'm going to do this shit on my own time and in my own way. Keep fucking with me, your ass gone end up missing. Do you understand?" I really wanted to answer, but my legs made a mistake and wrapped around his waist. All I wanted to do was help myself breathe a lil better, but his dick hardened under me and that caused my pussy to jump. Looking in his eyes, I could see them soften and I knew he wasn't mad anymore. Even though he went to snatch my pants down, his hand never left my neck.

It wasn't in a threatening way, so the shit started to turn me on. Pushing my legs apart with force, a moan escaped my lips. I knew I shouldn't be doing this, but I couldn't stop myself. His ass was fine as hell, and his sex appeal was intoxicating. He looked like the type that would warm you up with some head first, hell a finger or something. Instead, he shoved it in me with no preparation.

"Ahhhhhh." Screaming out from pain, I had to get adjusted to his size. My husband was about a strong six inches and I wasn't used to this kind of shit.

"Take this shit." His voice was low, and I could tell he was trying to keep his composure. This was his first piece of pussy in years and you could tell. This nigga was beating my shit up, and my pussy was begging for mercy. I couldn't tell if it felt good or if the shit hurt. Either way, my ass came all on that dick. Leaning down, he bit my lip and I could tell he was about to cum. That nigga snatched out and came all over my good clothes. I was ready to slap the shit out of his ass, but I was glad he didn't cum in me.

"Wow. This the shit you doing now? Our son die, and you turn into a hoe. You fucking this nigga where the entire neighborhood can see?" Hearing Franklin's voice had me embarrassed than a motherfucker. Jumping up, I pulled my clothes up as if he didn't already catch me with my pussy in the air.

"I'm no longer your concern. What are you doing here anyway?" Jaleel was fixing his self, but I could tell he was watching Franklin and I prayed he didn't do anything.

"After our talk, I felt bad for the shit I said. I was coming by to spend the night and to see if we could work on our problems. Silly me. You're working on shit already. Who is this thug wanna be?" Knowing this was about to go from bad to worse, I dropped my head. Jaleel didn't even respond, he just knocked him the fuck out.

"When homeboy wakes up, tell his ass it would be in his best interest to keep that shit moving. If he comes in this house on some bullshit, I will make that nigga go to sleep permanently." Walking to the door, I hurried up and unlocked it, so his ass could go the fuck on. Running back over to Franklin, I shook him until his ass came to. Now his ass looked more embarrassed than I did.

"What the hell is wrong with you Valencia? I know we lost our son, but this is not like you. You done brought this trash to our house and you expect me to be okay with this." This nigga must have had amnesia or something.

"Our house? Nigga was it our house when you moved out to go be with that bitch? Don't play with me. I can bring anybody in here I want to. Go home Franklin before he comes back out here." Standing up, he knocked the dust off his suit. Trying to hold in a laugh, I watched him walk towards the car stumbling. I'm sure it's been a long time since he felt a hit like that.

Looking around, I tried to make sure none of my neighbors were watching. When Franklin pulled off, I walked in the house not knowing what to say. Jaleel was walking around looking at the pictures on my wall. Not knowing what to say, I just stared at Shawn.

"Is this him? Your son."

"Yeah, that's him." Feeling myself getting emotional, I went to sit on my couch. I hated talking about him, but I needed Jaleel to do what he was here for. The sex was bomb, but I didn't give a fuck about none of that. If that's what it took to make him move forward with the plan, then I would do just that. His ass was still stuck on Pebbles, maybe this was my way of keeping him focused on the task at hand. Some people might call me a hoe, but I was a hoe that was about to get shit done.

"Go in the room and take that shit off. When I come in there I want you on your knees ready to suck this dick. It's been a while and it's going to be a long night for you and that pussy." Yeah I needed him to do something for me, but I was excited about the night we were about to have. It's been a long time since I got my shit played in as well. Sex wouldn't cloud my judgment, but my pussy jumped in excitement.

CHAPTER EIGHT SPADE

Laying here looking at Valencia, I wondered what her deal was. She seemed to be a pretty decent person, but she was about to hit a point of no return. Most people thought it was easy to kill someone, but when that shit ain't in you, it fucks with your mind. I remember the first time I killed someone, I couldn't sleep for weeks. I had a dream about his ass every night. It was like the nigga was haunting me.

I'm not sure if she was built for this kind of shit. If her ass was taken in for questioning, she would turn my ass in for a cup of soda and a bag of chips. After seeing Pebbles today, I had mixed emotions. I wanted to kill her just for having a baby with another nigga. She thought she was about to lay up with his ass, not today. I could hear her telling Tiana 'issa snack'. Now the bitch can eat his ass for breakfast.

Because I wasn't sure how I wanted to play this, I planned to follow her ass around. In the meantime, I would have a field day fucking with her ass. Nobody knew I was out and I knew it would fuck her head up for the shit I was about to bring her way. Knowing that Shvonne didn't get up until the afternoon, I decided to get a head start on her. Grabbing my phone, I called the prison I was housed out.

"Inmate information, Sheila speaking."

"Hello Sheila. My name is Jaleel Spade and I was just an inmate there. I have a proposition for you." It didn't take me long to convince Sheila of what I needed her to do. Money talks and I had plenty of that. Even though Shvonne thought she had it all, I was still caked up. If she had played her cards for a few more days, she definitely would have gotten it all.

Walking to the bathroom, I jumped in the shower. Once I was done, I took care of all my hygiene. Forgetting that I didn't have any damn clothes here, I shook my head as I had to put the same shit back on. As soon as the mall opened, I was going to hit that bitch up. Not wanting to be seen by anybody I knew, I was going to hit the one in Indiana. No matter how far you go out in Illinois, you always ran into somebody you knew. When niggas trying to creep, they go way out hoping they could stay on the low. Making sure Valencia was still sleep, I headed out to my stash house. First, I packed a duffle bag full of money. I didn't want to keep coming back here compromising my spot.

Second, I grabbed a few more guns and some ammo. Last but not least, I grabbed a pocket knife out of my case. My father had a case full of knives he collected. Since I always spaded a motherfucker, I kept the knives to use when I killed a nigga. Leaving out, I made my way to the warehouse.

Checking around, I made sure that Shvonne wasn't here. Sliding inside, her workers were damn near sleep. Making my presence known, I cleared my throat.

"King Spade what the fuck? Man I must be high as fuck. I need to quit hitting our product. I'm seeing shit Jo." The lil nigga looked spooked.

"Well, I must be fucked up as well cus I see that nigga too." Trying not to laugh, these niggas was tweaking like a motherfucker.

"Naw nigga, that's him. I'm sober as fuck and that nigga standing in my face smirking." Pulling my gun on the sober one, I smiled and pulled the trigger. Taking the rest of them out, I headed to the office to hit the safe. It was funny to me that she didn't change the pass code. I guess the cocky in her made her feel I would never be back home.

After emptying the contents of the safe, I went back to the front where the niggas were lying dead. Pulling my knife out, I did what I did best. Knowing that would fuck her head up, I left out. Jumping back into my moms car, I headed to the mall. Knowing it would be a few hours before Pebbles came, I could get me some well needed clothes and shoes. I would have sent Valencia, but her ass would have come back with some slacks and boat shoes.

After tearing the mall up, I headed back to the warehouse. When I pulled up, I was happy to know Shvonne's ass still wasn't there. Parking, I was there about thirty minutes before she pulled up. Smiling, I couldn't wait to see her face. Even though I wanted to walk in and let her know who the fuck I was, I knew it wasn't the time. I would let my presence be known when it was time. She fucked with my feelings for the longest, and I was about to return the fucking favor.

Shvonne came running out of the warehouse and I could tell she was fighting back throw up. Looking around, she was trying to see if anyone was out there. When she started rubbing her necklace, I was shocked she still had it. Jumping in her car, she drove off crying. That let me know she wasn't as tough as she liked to let on. There was no room for me to feel sorry for her ass though, one wrong emotion would have my ass back in her grasp. I needed to teach Shvonne a lesson. My feelings would have to be put on the back burner. Queen P was going down, she just didn't know it yet. Pulling off, I headed back to Valencia's house.

When I left, I made sure the door was unlocked. When I got back, the shit was locked. I knew Valencia was here because her car was still in the drive way. Ringing the bell, I was pissed the bitch had me waiting. She pulled the door open with an attitude.

"Where the fuck have you been? I got up to cook you breakfast and your ass was gone. You could have made sure I was awake before you just left up out of here." Bitch was nagging like she was my woman.

"I don't have to check in with you, and nobody told your ass to cook if you saw I was gone. I know this dick life changing, but don't get this shit twisted. I'm here for one reason only, not to be your nigga."

"You still love her don't you?" Not about to do that whining shit, I walked off and headed to the spare bedroom. I'm not sleeping with her ass again if this how the fuck she was going to act. The only reason I gave her the dick was because it's been a while since I hit some pussy. She was nowhere near my type and her pussy was borderline dry. Shit was mediocre, but it did the trick. All I needed was a nut, not a relationship.

Putting my clothes and shoes away, I knew I was going to need more, but this would do for now. A nigga couldn't be walking around looking regular and shit. I knew she was in the room before I turned around. Valencia had this eerie silence about herself. She seemed sincere, but you could tell it was a side to her you had to watch. I didn't trust her ass for shit, and I knew if I didn't do shit the way she wanted it done, I would have to give her ass a fade.

"I'm sorry. I don't know why I was acting like that. I know you're not my nigga, I just don't want her ass to play you again. If you let her, she will get in your mind. If she played you once, she will play you twice. Why put yourself through that shit?" Either I wasn't paying attention at first, or her ass went and changed. She was standing in front of me with some booty shorts on and that ass was spilling out. Not wanting to talk about Pebbles, I decided to give the corn starch pussy another try. One thing I learned from being in jail was, bad pussy is better than no pussy. I just needed to grab some condoms. My dick was going to be chaffed if I kept going up in that shit raw.

CHAPTER NINE SHVONNE

My ass was starting to stress the fuck out and I needed to get it together. I couldn't allow my soldiers to sense fear even though I was scared. I've never had anyone directly try to kill me, and now that I have Jelly I have to think about her. Getting dressed, I got myself together to head to the warehouse. I needed to have a meeting with my crew. This type of shit couldn't happen again.

Before me, nobody even thought about going at Spade. That's how I knew they were coming at me because I was a woman. They thought I wasn't as vicious as Spade could be. That notion was about to end today, I couldn't have niggas thinking it was cool to come to my crib. That was the one thing I should have kept separate, but I was being lazy as hell. Once I was done getting ready, I grabbed my keys and headed out. Driving towards the warehouse, I knew it was going to be a good day.

Nothing made me feel better than reminding a motherfucker I was the queen around here. Making sure my gun was loaded, I smiled as I got out and walked inside the warehouse. My soul shook out my body looking at the scene before me. Not only was everybody dead, but they had been spaded.

"There is no way. No. No. No. How the fuck was he out? There is no way Spade can be out." My ass was walking in circles talking to myself. Trying to control my emotions, I rubbed my hands down my suit jacket. As if taking the wrinkles away was going to make my problems disappear. Leaving out of the warehouse, I jumped back in my car with tears in my eyes.

Needing to know if Spade was out, or if someone was fucking with me I drove to the prison. The entire way there, my hands shook. If this nigga was out, that changed everything. I didn't know who my crew would roll with. Well the niggas that I had left. It wasn't many, but their loyalty may still be to Spade. As scared as I was, a part of me felt some kind of excitement. Even though I didn't want to, I loved him, and his sex was off the chain.

In another life, he would have been the perfect man. No matter how I tried to turn the shit, I had to avenge Bam. How could I fall for the nigga that took him away from me? That was something I would never be able to wrap my mind around. Bam was my everything and Spade gunned him down like he wasn't shit. Granted, Bam was about to shoot his ass, but still. I wasn't with Spade, and I was rolling with my nigga from the streets to the grave. Pulling up, I parked my car and my nerves were all over the place. My phone ringing scared the shit out of me. Seeing it was Tiana, I damn near broke my finger I answered so fast. I prayed nothing else was wrong.

"Hey T, what's up? Is Jelly good?"

"Yeah, but she woke up screaming for you. Where are you?" Not wanting to get into it over the phone, I kept it short.

"Some shit popped off and I'm at the prison visiting Spade. I'm about to walk in and I will talk to you when I get home."

"Wait Spade. What the fuck?" Hanging up, I was not about to do this with her ass. She would ask a million questions if I let her. Knowing I needed to find out what was going on, I got my ass out of the car and headed inside. After going through all the checkpoints, I finally made it to the desk to get the info I needed. The lady looked like she had an attitude, but I didn't care. She was going to talk to me today.

"Excuse me, I'm trying to visit Jaleel Spade. Is he still an inmate here?" The bitch didn't even look up, she just kept typing in her computer.

"What's your name?" Rolling my eyes, I wanted to slap her in the mouth. She never answered my damn question.

"Shvonne Lavigne." Typing some more, she finally looked up.

"I'm sorry. Jaleel has refused all of your visits. You can't see him today. If you think it is an error, talk to Jaleel and have him put in another request. I'm sorry." She thought I was upset about not being able to see him. Little did she know, if he would've walked his ass out them doors, I was running towards the nearest exit. That was something I wasn't ready to do.

"It's okay. Thank you." A bitch damn near skipped to my car. I damn near screamed out skip to the trap my darling. Laughing at my own joke, I threw my shades on and drove the fuck off. That would be the last time I would ever see this place. I needed to put Spade behind me and I couldn't do that if I kept letting that nigga live rent free in my shit. I done drove my scary ass all the way out here for nothing. Knowing damn well his ass wasn't out, I done let my nerves get the best of me.

Realizing that it wasn't Spade, somebody was fucking with me and I needed to find out who it was as soon as possible. Knowing how I set up Spade, I knew how the game went. It could be anybody friend or foe. Karma was trying to rear her ugly ass face, but I beat all bitches up. I don't give a fuck what that hoe was trying to do, it wasn't gone happen on my time.

Pulling up to my house, I headed inside. All I did was drive to the prison, but I was exhausted. Too much thinking and I still had no idea who the fuck was after me. Right now, all I wanted to see was my baby, I needed to feel some love. Walking in her room, I noticed she wasn't there. Panic started to hit me, and I took off screaming through the house. Her and Tiana finally came out of the back yard looking at me like I was crazy as hell. Seeing that everything was fine, I grabbed Jelly and hugged her.

"What the hell wrong with you and why were you visiting HIM?" After I gave my baby a million kisses, I answered.

"Somebody took out the crew this morning and spaded them. I had to make sure it wasn't him. He is still locked up, but that means somebody is fucking with me. His ass probably got somebody out here doing his dirty work. If it's a war he wants, then it's a war he is going to get." Tiana looked at me in disbelief.

"Do you hear yourself? You set that man up, you didn't tell him about her, and you took all his shit. You don't feel a little bit of remorse? You got people after you and you're still trying to live this life. When is it going to be enough?" This bitch had a lot of nerve.

"You sitting your ass up on this high horse and you seem to be forgetting that you helped me do all the shit you're claiming I did. Your hands are just as dirty as mine. Don't stand here and judge me."

"Nobody is trying to judge you best friend, but the shit is old and tired. We did what we did but look at you. I can tell you're scared as hell. You have enough money, we can walk away from this shit. It's not worth the risk. You have Jelly to think about. Maybe he will call them off if he knew about her." This bitch was about to piss me off.

"Tiana, what is it going to change if he knows about her? Not a damn thing. All that is going to do is give him more fucked up thoughts about me. I took him away from his child. Granted, I didn't know I was pregnant when I did the shit, but the damage is done. I have to live with the decisions I made. We both do. Don't try to clear your conscience now."

"Whatever. Nobody can tell you shit, but when your mistakes cause you to lose this lil girl you love so much, remember what the fuck I said. You can keep pretending to them out there that you're this strong ass bitch, but I know you." This hoe had the nerve to walk off from me.

I got what she was trying to say, but it was too late for all that now. She wanted me to wipe the slate clean, but there was no way Spade would forgive me. I did what I did out of love, I just didn't expect to have feelings or a baby.

That shit was dead. I had bigger problems to worry about now. I needed to find out who was after me before the shit came back to my front door. Jelly was my first priority, being Queen P was the second. I had to figure out how to balance it before my shit came crumbling down.

"Come on Jelly you get to make your mommy lunch today." When she smiled my heart melted. She looked just like Spade, it was hard to forget about a nigga you had to see every day.

CHAPTER TEN VALENCIA

Walking into the office, I was wore the hell out. My pussy wasn't used to getting all this attention and me and Jaleel were going at it like rabbits. I was happy as hell he got some condoms, because my ass wasn't trying to get pregnant. Especially not by him. His sex was great, but not good enough to sway me from our deal. Jaleel thought he was slick, his ass thought good sex would have me gone in the head and make me change my mind. We had a deal and if he tried to change up, his ass would pay.

"Brolen, in my office now." My Boss always acted as if he had a stick up his ass, but it seemed like he was pissed today. Walking as slow as I could, I finally made it inside and closed the door. Taking a seat, I wondered what the hell he wanted.

"What the fuck is this shit?" Slamming Jaleel's paperwork down on the desk, I could feel the sweat running down my forehead. I was hoping no one would even notice.

"There was a technicality with his arrest. We had to release him. By law, I had to do my job once I realized what happened." Fire was coming out of his eyes he was so mad. Praying I wouldn't get fired, I held my breath waiting on him to respond.

"Fuck a technicality. You have the Mayor breathing down my neck asking for answers. Why didn't you come to me first before you did this shit? Your enthusiasm has brought down a shit storm on this office."

"I'm sorry. You know I go by the book. By law, I had to do what was right. If he is what they say he is, we will get him again. You or the Mayor can't ask me to do underhanded shit. That's not what I signed up for."

"Do you think the Mayor gives a fuck about your morals? I don't care what you have to do, your ass have one month to get his ass back in that cell or that's your ass. Figure out some type of legal way you can arrest him again or set his ass up. Either way, you better get him back."

Waving me off, I knew he was done with this conversation. Not even stopping at my desk, I grabbed my purse and went back to the house. I needed Jaleel to do this shit fast. If I had to find a way to lock him up, I needed him to do this job as soon as possible. Hoping he hadn't left yet, I drove fast as hell. Seeing his car still there, I jumped out and headed inside. He was still in bed, and I woke his ass up with a slap across the chest.

"Jaleel, get up. We need to talk." His jaw line started jumping and I knew his ass was pissed. He been sleeping in the guest room and I have no idea why. We always end up fucking, so you would think he would just stay in my room.

"Don't get fucked up. All the fuck you do is whine, what do you want?"

69

"When are you going to handle our little problem? You've had plenty of time to do what you need to do, but you're procrastinating. Just kill the bitch already." Sitting up on the bed, he looked at me with fire in his eyes. I knew he was about to go off.

"Are you slow or something? For real, do you have trouble comprehending or some shit? I told you I was going to do the shit on my own time, yet; you're still in my fucking face asking me the same fucking questions."

"I hear your ass loud and clear, but I'm not buying the shit. I know you had plenty of opportunities to do it. What the fuck are you waiting on? You have a few weeks to do this shit, or the deal is off." The nigga actually laughed at me.

"You already signed the papers. Whether I do the shit or not, you can't send me back. Now get the fuck out of my face before you get your feelings hurt."

"The same way I got you out, I can put your ass back in. Fuck with me if you want to. You're a killer, but I have the system. Think about that why you out here throwing threats." Jumping up, he grabbed me by my neck cutting off everything. A bitch could barely swallow, let alone spit.

"Are you threatening me? I promise you don't want to go down this road. I'm asking your ass to let me do me, but if I have to do it again, the shit won't be good for you." Finally getting his hands from around my neck, I shivered at who was before me. His eyes were cold as hell. I didn't give a fuck though, I needed him to do our plan before I got his ass sent back to prison. If he didn't go back, I would lose my job.

Jaleel will be crossed by yet another bitch in his life, but this time it was do or die. One of us were going to be on the line, and it would not be me. Leaving out of the room, I headed to my study to look at law books. I was trying to find some type of legal precedence to put his ass back in jail. Once he did what I needed him to do, I really didn't give a fuck what happened to him.

For two hours, I did a lot of talking to myself and going the fuck off. I don't think it was a legal way for me to lock Jaleel back up. Knowing I may need to do something drastic, I pulled out my work files. I went over everything I knew about Pebbles, and I went over Jaleel's case with a fine tooth comb. It was something I was missing and the shit was starting to frustrate me.

The shit had to be right in my face, but my eyes were burning trying to find it. Knowing I needed to take a break from it, I put everything away and walked out of my office. Going into the kitchen, I poured myself a drink. Leaning my head back, I took a deep breath trying to ease the pressure in my mind.

Out of nowhere, it hit me. If I had to set Jaleel up, I knew exactly how to do it. Running back to my office, I pulled out Pebble's file again. Yes, this would definitely work. I have been following Jaleel for the most part, I knew exactly how to pull this off if it came down to it. I really didn't want to turn into that person, but if Jaleel didn't do what I needed, I would be forced to take matters into my own hands. Smiling to myself, I headed to my bedroom. Neither one of them would know what hit they ass. When I walked in my room, Jaleel was standing there looking at me.

"What the fuck are you up to Valencia?" Feeling like a pubic hair caught in a zipper, I didn't know what to say. Thinking of a lie, I tried to play it cool.

"I am a State's Attorney that has a job to do. The shit with Pebbles is off the record, but if you're not trying to pay my bills I have to work." He stared at me as if he wasn't buying it.

"After the shit with Pebbles, I don't trust a bitch with my balls. You have this sneaky look going on and my instincts are telling me not to trust your ass. Don't try to cross me." Not even giving me a chance to explain any further, he walked out leaving me looking stupid. His ass can guess all he wants to, but at the end of the day, him and his bitch was going down. Whenever I'm given a choice to save me or the next motherfucker, I'm going to choose myself every time. Lying in my bed, I was about to go to bed and sleep good knowing I had a plan.

CHAPTER ELEVEN HALLE

Driving towards my mama's house, I had a lot on my mind. Since Bruno been home, shit ain't been the same. Part of the problem was us not knowing much about each other. After the night in the club, we started fucking like two jack rabbits. We barely saw each other because he was always doing something for Spade. I used to think it was the dopest shit ever.

Me cooking dinner and sitting around naked for him to come over. His ass would be all over me after eating one of my bomb ass meals. It would be late as hell, but I catered to his ass. We would have sex, lay up, and talk shit until it was time for him to head back to the warehouse. It almost seemed as if he lived here with me. I was enjoying that shit.

Now, shit is different. We can see all the shit you're supposed to notice about a person when you're dating. We're here with each other all day, and I hate the shit. That only made me hate Pebbles more. If it wasn't for her, that nigga would barely be here, and we would still be living the perfect lie. When you're up under a person, you start to notice shit you never saw before. In the beginning, shit seems perfect. Everyone goes through that honeymoon faze, but when that shit is over, you may end up realizing you don't even like that motherfucker.

Bruno was one lazy nigga. It's like he doesn't want to do shit if it's not concerning the streets. The nigga finds a way to turn anything I ask him to do about business. Hey baby, I'm tired can you cook today? I can cook up some dope, I'm nice as fuck with that shit. Hey Bruno, can you take out the trash? I wish I could take that bitch Pebbles out. Nigga was getting on my last nerve and I needed some advice.

A part of me wanted to take Pebbles out because this shit was her fault, but that shit wasn't going to happen with the army she has behind her. A bitch had to hate her silently, you never knew who she was affiliated with. At this moment, the bitch thought she was untouchable, but every dog has its day. Last I checked, that bitch was barking. She didn't realize that all the shit she did to people would come back to bite her in the ass one day, but she will. That's the way of the world. What goes around, comes back around and I was going to be front and center when her shit came full circle. Pulling up to my mama's house, I got out of my car and headed up to the door. Using my key, I walked in and my mama was sitting on the couch.

"Look what the cat drug in. I thought you forgot you had a mama. Haven't seen you in months. That tells me it's something you want. How much is it?" This was the reason I stayed away. Whenever I came by, she treated me like I was some begging ass bitch off the streets. We've always had a complicated relationship. I didn't go away to school like she wanted, so anytime I needed her help, she refused to give it to me.

"Mama, I don't need anything I just needed to talk. If you gone do all that, I can just leave." Rolling her eyes, she lit up a cigarette.

"Girl, stop being so damn sensitive. If you came to talk, then quit all the melodramatic shit and talk. You always do that shit, acting like somebody supposed to be able to read your mind. Your head too small for that shit." Sitting down, I decided to talk since I came over here.

"You remember Pebbles? She basically switched it up on us and took the job from my man. Now his ass sitting around, and he won't do shit. I'm tired and I need to know what to do."

"You shouldn't have been running behind her anyway. I've learned a long time ago that no man or woman was worth me chasing. That would make them better than me. You can't be mad at her for doing what she does. In this world, you just have some of those kind of people." I knew what she was saying was the truth, but that's not the answer I was looking for.

"Every time I look at my life, I want to kill her ass. She played me like I wasn't shit. I let that girl live with me when she first moved here. Helped her do all kinds of shit and she had the nerve to talk to me like I was nothing." My mama nodded her head like she understood.

75

"You must get that shit from your father. That girl treated you like you were beneath her since she met you. She was just a lil nicer because she needed you. Either way, just move on with your life. Karma will get her in the end. I promise you won't have to do shit to her. Focus on that no good ass bed bug you got on your couch."

"Why you calling him a bed bug mama? Bruno is fine."

"Bed bugs latch on to whoever sits they ass in their space. Suck them dry and then move on to the next person. As soon as you are no help to that boy, he will leave you. Mark my words."

"I hear you ma. I'm going to get out of here. I need to go home and cook." As if she knew I was rushing home to Bruno, she shook her head at me. Leaving out, I realized I learned nothing. I was still just as pissed at Pebbles, and my dumb ass was still going home to make sure Bruno was straight. I could have stayed in the house and avoided the bitch you dumb as hell looks from my mom.

Jumping in my car, I rushed to the grocery store. Grabbing some chicken breasts, potatoes, and broccoli I headed home to get dinner started. Maybe I just wanted things to get better, and I felt if I did my part then he would do his. All he needed was something to do, and we would be back on the right track. Thinking of a plan, I rushed home to tell Bruno about it.

When I pulled up, I damn near broke my ankle trying to get in the house. Stepping inside, he was sitting in his same spot on the couch with a bottle of D'usse half empty at his feet. Meek Mills Dreams and Nightmares was blasting on the speakers and if I wasn't so disgusted, I would have turned the fuck up. That was my shit, but I needed Bruno to get out of this damn funk. Walking over to the speakers, I turned it off.

"What the fuck you do that for? I'm not trying to argue today and I'm not in the mood for your shit." Rolling my eyes, I sat across from him.

"While I was out, I thought about our problem. Instead of trying to get the organization from Pebbles, why not start our own. Get a crew and take hers down. She has no real backing if Spade is not behind her. All we have to do is take the shit from her. That's if the old Bruno is still in there somewhere. Or we can do it your way, and just sit at home complaining about the bitch every twenty minutes." You could see him thinking it over.

"Bitch don't think I didn't feel that shade your ass just threw, but I think you're up to something. Pebbles doesn't have any real backing. She losing niggas left and right. Somebody else is after her too and that helps us. As long as they aren't after the empire, we should be good."

"We know her routine Bruno, and we know where she lives. All we have to do is take her out. If you're worried about the crew coming after us, then we build a crew first. The shit shouldn't be that hard. I lived with her for a few years. It's easy as hell to take from a motherfucker. We can rob her traps and she will blame them. When they are at their weakest point, we can take her out. It's all on the way you want to do it, but it can be done."

"Why the fuck it take you so long to think about that shit? This what the fuck I'm talking about. I got with you because I thought you was a down ass chick. Your ass been off your shit since I been home, but you back now. She will never know what hit her ass and I'm ready for it. When it comes down to it, your ass better not punk out either. You know you scared of that bitch."

"I'm not scared of her or you either. Don't fucking play with me Bruno. I'm ready as soon as you are, fuck that bitch."

"Then it's on. It's time out for games. Now go in there and start dinner, so you can get in here and suck this dick." Smiling, I walked off to the kitchen. Me and Bruno was going to be okay. All I needed to do was give him a purpose, now we can be the power couple I knew we could be.

CHAPTER TWELVE SPADE

After Valencia went to work, I headed to her office. That bitch was up to something and I needed to figure out what it was. There was no way I would ever trust her, no matter what the fuck she said. The only reason I agreed to stay here was to watch her and make sure she didn't try shit. The sex was just something to do.

A nigga was locked up for years and at this point, any pussy would do. Her shit wasn't even good, but it was enough to get me a nut. Not wanting to risk somebody seeing me, I didn't want to go fuck a random. I wasn't ready to let Pebbles know I was out just yet, but the time was coming. Since I was a flashy nigga, I wanted to do something drastic. When it came to me, I would know the exact thing to do in order to get her attention.

I have been fucking with her damn near every day, but I slacked off a little trying to watch what was going on. She had crossed a lot of people and the shit was going to bite her in the ass. Knowing I wanted to be on my shit when I finally came face to face with her, I left out of Valencia's house to go pick up my moms. There was some shit I needed her to do for me. Knowing she was going to talk shit, I prepared myself before I got there. She did the most at times, but she always had my back. When I pulled up, she was chasing some nigga down the driveway with a bat.

Not knowing what he did, I grabbed my strap and twisted on the silencer. Letting my window down, it took me one shot to take his ass out. Pulling into the driveway, I parked and got out. My mama was looking at me with an expression I couldn't read.

"What the fuck is wrong with you? You done killed the number one nigga on my roster. Did I kill your bitch when I knew she wasn't shit? I should slap the shit out of your ass. Best sex I done had in years and now he bleeding all over the damn concrete. Who gone clean this shit up?" Knowing we didn't allow people in our homes, I was confused.

"What the fuck is wrong with you? I saw you chasing the nigga and I handled it. We don't let people know where we live, so I thought your ass was in trouble."

"I am in trouble. Philip popped up on my ass and Fred is in the house. My ass was out there picking a fight to get him to leave. I didn't want his ass dead. Fred cooks and eat my pussy before a meal. Philip is just to blow my back out. Now look what the fuck you done did." Knowing I didn't want to hear that shit, I went to pick up his body so I could put it in the trunk. If I called the clean up crew, they would know I was out.

"Ma, you really need to gone head on with that shit. You too old to be talking like that. Come help me clean this shit up before somebody see this shit." Slapping me in the head, she walked over to grab him.

"Janice what the fuck. You killed my brother, I'm about to kill your ass. You stupid bitch, why did you kill my brother?" This guy I'm assuming is Fred came outside screaming. My moms was looking embarrassed, but I needed to end the shit before he drew attention. Pulling my gun, I shot his ass too.

"Ma, you nasty as fuck. You around here fucking brothers. That shit ain't right. Hurry up and grab this nigga so we can get his ass next. I didn't come over here for this shit. I'm trying to stay under the radar."

"Once upon a time not long ago I was a hoe. Ain't that how that song go. Yaasssss. Son, your mama ain't shit. Leel might not even be your daddy. Don't look at me like that, you still got their blood. Unless it was the gardener. I did slip up with him one night Leel didn't come home." Looking at her in disbelief, she laughed at me. "You're right, that's neither here nor there. All that matters is what you believe. Now, I believe you done killed both of my niggas. You owe me a dip off."

Not responding to her, I threw the guy in the trunk. Jumping in the car, I drove towards her door and got out. Grabbing the other nigga, I threw his ass in as well. All I wanted to do was come over here and handle some business, now I was tired as fuck.

"I'm going to drop you off at the car lot. I need you to purchase you another car and get one for me. Tell the guy you will be back to pick up the second car. I have to get rid of this one and then I'll call you to come get me. Don't do no more stupid shit like this again. Shit was reckless and uncalled for. You too old for the dumb shit." Climbing in the car with me, she slammed the door and looked at me as if I lost my mind.

"Well what the fuck was you when that bitch played you and took everything all the way down to the fish in your floor? She probably over there having a fish fry as we speak. You get a fish, you get a fish, you and your mama get a fish. Dumb ass, now you wanna talk shit. Fuck you, drive." Not about to feed into her shit, I drove as fast as I could to the car lot. Lucky for us, we had a nigga that we dealt with there and didn't have to worry about questions.

Grabbing the money, she got out and slammed the door again. I think she forgot it was her car. Well, it was her car this bitch was about to go up in flames as soon as I got to a safe location. Making sure to not draw attention from the police, I stopped at a gas station then went to a spot that me and the homies used to take bodies to all the time. Putting a towel in the tank, I lit the bitch and got the fuck out of dodge. Once I was at a safe distance, I watched until the car was no more. Walking until I got back to the street, I called my moms and gave her my location. It took her a little over an hour and she finally came. I should have known she would be extra as hell with my money. The Tesla was nice, but it would have been real nice if I hadn't paid for it. Not saying a word, I got in and she took me back to the lot.

"Where the rest of my money ma? I know you didn't spend it all on the cars, I need you to go furnish my house." When she laughed in my face, I knew I was gone have to come up off some more money.

"Did you get your money back from that bitch? Oh okay. Then I'm going to need some more money." She handed me my car keys, and I climbed out of the car.

"Just do it ma and I'll give back what you spent. I need you to do it today though." Not giving her a chance to respond, I closed the door and walked towards my car. Happy she got me a Maserati, I climbed in and felt at home. Thanks to my moms, I knew I was going to need some more money. The first thing I did was head back to the stash house. Grabbing some more cash, headed to the store. I needed some new items, and I had to go way out to get them. Trying to keep from being seen was harder than I thought it would be. Being King Spade wasn't a small thing. Niggas swore on my life every day.

The only motherfucker who didn't honor who the fuck I was is Pebbles. If her target wasn't me, I would have been impressed. Instead, I was thinking of ways to fuck with her before I finally took her out. If I was being honest with myself, it was me actually trying to see if I could. Once I had all the items I needed, I jumped in my car and pulled off with a smile. Shit was about to get real.

CHAPTER THIRTEEN SHVONNE

Shutting down the warehouse was not something I wanted to do, but until I figured out what the fuck was going on I didn't want to put anybody else in jeopardy. I damn sure didn't want to put myself in harm's way. Everything was falling apart, and I didn't know how to deal with it.

From the moment I found out I was pregnant, I held regrets on the shit I did. I couldn't change the past and I had to accept the shit. Regardless of how I felt about Spade, in my heart I thought I owed it to Bam to avenge his death. Now, I'm not sure the shit was worth it. My baby girl needed me and now I feared for her life. If I knew who was after us, I could handle that shit and move on. How the fuck do you fight an enemy you can't see?

"Pebbles, I know you hear me calling you bitch. Where the fuck your head at?" Turning to Tiana, I had to bite my tongue. She's been getting real slick at the mouth blaming me for all the shit that's going on. I know it was my fault, but I didn't want to hear the shit every five minutes. If Jelly didn't want her ass with us, I would have left her at home. I'm trying to deal with the shit the best way I knew how, I didn't need someone constantly telling me I fucked up. If she wasn't my best friend, I would have been hurt her feelings.

"I don't know. Just thinking, find anything you like?" Regardless of her smart ass comments, I wouldn't be able to do shit if it wasn't for her. Tiana was an absolute God send when it came to Jelly. That's why I said okay when Jelly asked her to come. She deserved this shopping spree.

"Bitch did I. Your ass about to be mad when we hit that counter. You done bought the entire store out for Jelly I see. That baby do not need all that shit." When I looked down at all the stuff I had, all I could do was laugh. I did go overboard.

"Her daddy was a flashy nigga and you already know how I dress. It's only right that our baby matches our fly." When she looked at me and smiled, I was confused.

"Why the fuck you smiling like we in jail and they just locked me in the room with your ass?" Falling out laughing, she slapped me on the arm and I kicked her in the shin. Jelly hit me on my booty trying to help Tiana.

"That's right TT's baby, help your auntie. I'm smiling because this was the first time you reference Spade as being the father. It might be some hope that you will tell him after all." Ignoring what she said about Spade, I grabbed Jelly and bit her jaw.

"You going against your mommy for your auntie? I'm not buying you anymore candy."

"That's okay, your auntie got a drawer full for you." Paying for the stuff, we walked out in a great mood.

"Where y'all want to eat? It's all about y'all today. If it was up to me, my ass would be at Harold's Chicken." They knew I loved Harold's mild sauce and I could eat that shit every day.

"Let's go to Home Run Inn. I haven't had pizza in a long time. I'm sure Jelly tired of eating all that fancy food her mama likes aren't you baby?" My damn child betrayed me again.

"Pissa. Pissa." Laughing, I agreed to the pizza and we walked out the door. Times like this make me wish Spade could be here to witness it. I never thought I would be a single mom, and I never would have wanted that for my child. Hell, I never expected to be pregnant by Spade. After the first child I lost, I was too afraid to lose another one. Happy that I kept my baby, I looked at her smiling. She was holding my hand so tight and talking to Tiana at the same time. She held both of our hearts and even without a father, I thought she was a lucky little girl.

Pft Pft Pft... Gunshots rang out before I could do anything. Dropping my body on top of Jelly's, I prayed she would be okay. It seemed like the shots went off forever. Once they stopped, I jumped up to make sure Jelly was good.

"Owee mommy." Tears fell down my face as I laughed. This lil girl was oblivious to what the fuck happened, and we needed to get the hell out of there. "TT sweepy."

"What?" Looking behind me, saw Tiana was still down on the ground. "No. No. No. This is not happening. Tiana get up best friend." When I saw how many times she got hit, my hope dwindled. Grabbing my phone, I called 911. Praying Tiana was okay, I held Jelly's face in my chest. I tried my best to be strong, but my heart was breaking. Not wanting my baby to see Tiana like that, I continued to rock her. The ambulance finally got there, and I waited until they loaded her up. Once I found out what hospital they were taking her to, me and Jelly jumped in my car.

My nerves were shot on the way to the hospital, but I was trying to stay calm. Jelly had no idea what she just witnessed, and I was thankful for that. Not knowing what to expect, we parked and got out of the car. It felt like my legs were dragging as I walked inside. As soon as I walked to the desk, my nerves kicked in like a motherfucker. The nurse asked me to take a seat and someone would be to talk to me. Usually it took a long time for the doctors to come and update the family, but not today. His ass was there in fifteen minutes.

"I'm sorry, but Tiana died on the way to the hospital. The techs tried to revive her numerous of times. It was nothing we could do for her. I can say she didn't suffer long and hopefully that heals your heart a little. We can give you the information to some places you can use to handle her arrangements. If you want to see the body, they are cleaning her up now and you can go in once they are done." Not being able to hold it anymore, I let out a scream. Jelly started crying because I was, and she had no idea what was

87

going on. The doctor left us to cope and I waited to go back and see her.

The room was eerily quiet and that alone broke me down. Looking at her laying peacefully, gave me some type of comfort in my heart. She had been through so much, but I was happy to have saved her from that hell. The only thing I regretted was wasting so much time staying away from her. If I had known what she was going through, I would have flown her out sooner.

Jelly kept trying to climb on top of her and I had no idea what to say to her. She loved Tiana and even though she didn't understand death, this lost would affect her terribly. No matter how much I tried not to, the tears continued to fall. It was taking me through Bam's death all over again. I had no idea how she would have wanted to be buried. I this shit was too much, and I felt myself about to break all the way down. Knowing I needed to get out of there for now, I grabbed Jelly off of Tiana.

"Come on TT. Pissa." It felt like the breath left my body and I couldn't take it. Not being able to control my breathing, I tried my best to explain it to her.

"TT is going to be with the angels. Come on we have to go now." She cried because her TT couldn't go, but my heart was literally shattering. Guilt took over me as we got in the car and drove to my house. She tried to tell me to end this shit, but I was too stubborn. If I had gone and talked to Spade like she told me, people would not be after me. There was no way he would have people trying to kill me if he knew that I had his daughter.

Spade has now killed the only two people I had left and loved the most. After being honest with myself, both deaths were my fault. If I hadn't popped off with Spade, him and Bam's argument probably wouldn't have went that far. Tiana had been begging me to end this shit and talk to Spade and I wouldn't listen. My daughter could have been shot, and I would not have been able to handle that. I literally couldn't take shit else, and it was time to end this. I don't know how Spade would feel, but I was going to write him and ask him to put me on the list. However the shit went, it was time for us to have a sit down.

I knew he would be pissed, but my feelings were warranted. Pulling up to the house, I grabbed Jelly and headed inside. As soon as I walked in, I knew some shit was off. The goosebumps stood up on my arm, but before I could react a hand was placed over my mouth and everything went black.

CHAPTER FOURTEEN SPADE

I've been doing a lot to get shit set up for tonight. It was time for me to let my presence be known and I was ready to see Pebbles. I was tired of that behind the scenes shit, I was the fucking King and Motherfuckers needed to know can't nobody take me down. All the scheming she did, I was right here and able to take her fucking life.

Sitting inside her house, I waited to hear her car pull up. As soon as I did, I got in position and waited for the door to open. She walked in looking like she was barely making it. That shit pulled at my heart strings, but I had to try and stay focused. Yeah, I was probably the reason she was all fucked up, but it nowhere near compared to the shit she did to me. Placing the towel over her face, I waited until she passed out.

Not wanting the lil girl to make me feel like shit, I hit her nose with a little chloroform. Not wanting to harm her, I made sure she only inhaled a lil bit. Placing them both in the car, I drove towards my moms house. I needed her to keep Pebble's baby until I handled this situation. As fucked up as I was, I didn't want to harm the baby. That shit wasn't my thing, kids had a way of softening a nigga.

Pulling up to my mom's house, I carried the baby to her door. I knew Pebbles would be out for a while, so I wasn't worried.

My moms answered, and you could see confusion all on her face. She had no idea who this was, and I wasn't trying to get into it right now.

"When the fuck did you have a baby? Why are you bringing her to my house? Nigga who the fuck is her mama?" Shaking my head, she just couldn't be normal.

"Ma, this is not my baby. I need you to keep her for a lil while. I'm sure you can use the company since you lost your niggas. Be nice and I'll call you with what to do next." Reality set in and her head turned like the exorcist.

"You done kidnapped somebody's child? All hell no, get this fifteen to twenty ass case up out of my house. I'm too old to be in jail. They would take my shit and make me give them my cornbread. Son, you know I like cornbread. Why the fuck would you do that to your mama? Do all you can for your child and this how his tooty booty ass do you." Laughing, I walked out the door and left her to get acquainted with her new friend. Jumping back in the car, I headed to my house.

****

Pebbles finally started to stir around, and I knew she would wake up soon. I must admit, she still had the ability to get my dick hard on sight. Trying to stay focused, I stayed in the corner waiting on her to realize where she was. I didn't want her to see me just yet. I could see her eyes come all the way open and then damn near fall out of her head.

"What the fuck. Please, let me out of here. I plan on talking to Spade. It's something I need to tell him. Please don't do this. Where is my daughter? Please don't hurt my baby. Please." The last please was a just above a whisper, and the tears began to fall. I knew not to fall for that shit, and she wasn't about to pull me in with the dramatics. Trying to untie herself, she broke down harder when she realized it was nothing she could do. Finally ready to put her out of her misery, I walked slowly out of the corner.

"Hello Shvonne." I could literally see her heart stop beating.

"Spade? What the fuck." Smiling, I sat down in front of her. "Untie me right fucking now. You killed my best friend. I hate you, I fucking hate you. Why would you do that to me? How the fuck could you do that to me twice? Give me back my daughter, you better not hurt her. Please Spade, don't hurt her." The tears were coming uncontrollably, but I could no longer trust her, so I sat and listened. One thing I did learn from my father was, if you let a person talk, you could learn a lot without saying a word.

"Okay, listen. I was just about to come and talk to you. I'm sorry for everything I did. I honestly regretted it after, but it was too late. The deed was done, and I didn't know how to come to you. If I did, you know you wouldn't have wanted to hear it. Your life was gone because of me. I did have feelings for you, but I didn't know how to allow myself to love you and stay true to Bam. When you killed him, you took the biggest piece of my heart. Even though I know you don't care to hear it, I really am sorry." Getting up, I poured me a drink. Taking a sip, I thought about what I wanted to say first.

"Where is my money and cars?" You could tell she was hurt, but I wasn't about to address that other shit.

"I promise I will take you to it. All you have to do is untie me, I don't care about none of that shit, just give me my baby." I laughed so hard, liquor came out of my nose. The shit burned, and I had to regroup. I was here to kill her and damn near took my own self out laughing.

"You're going to tell me where my money is. I will never give you the chance to cross me twice."

"It's at my house in the basement. You won't see it, but it's a false floor. Push the button under the chair at my desk, it will lift the floor. We're even now, can we be done with this?" Not answering, I locked the basement and drove to her house. I wasn't with the bullshit anymore. When I pulled up, I made sure no one saw me lingering around her house. I didn't want to be affiliated with her disappearance at all. Going exactly where she told me to, I followed her instructions and the floor lifted.

There was all my money and a bunch of drugs. Putting the floor back down, I headed back to my house. I would get it another day, but right now I needed to handle this shit with Pebbles. Before I could get in my door, my moms called.

"Ma, I'm kind of in the middle of something. Let me call you back."

"Son, why the fuck didn't you tell me you had a fucking baby? Who is her mother? It must be some bitch straight out of the damn flea market for you to hide it. Who in the fuck gets swap meet pussy pregnant? Your ass just ain't gone learn. You have the worse taste in women. Just government assistant teeth having bitches." This lady was crazy as hell.

"Ma, I don't have no damn kids. Everybody that's light skinned don't look alike. I'm busy and I will call you back. I'll pay you for keeping her damn. Just keep her company until I come pick her up." Sometimes shit was aggravating the way she went on and on. Like damn, can you be serious sometimes?

"Nigga don't catch no attitude with me. I know you yellow niggas are sensitive, but this is your baby. She looks just like your ass." Not wanting to argue any longer, I left it alone.

"Okay ma. I'll call you back to talk about it." Hanging up, I shook my head and went inside. Grabbing my gun and my knife, I headed to my basement. Shit was about to get interesting for Queen P. Laughing, I walked in to seal her fate.

CHAPTER FIFTEEN HALLE

Lying on the floor, I cried as I tried to figure out how the fuck I got here. Everybody treated me like some weak bitch and I was tired of it. Being loyal or a down as bitch doesn't make me weak, the motherfucker who tries to take advantage of that shit is the weak one. Bruno just beat my ass because shit didn't go as planned. We had been following Pebbles, but my plan didn't work. Now I'm sitting here trying to figure out how the shit became my fault.

"Baby everything is falling into place. All of her soldiers are damn near out of the way. Now is the time to strike. We should take Pebbles out while she is vulnerable." Bruno was taking in everything I was saying. You could tell he was thinking it over.

"Now is not the time to be doing stupid shit. The bitch not even trying to build her team up. It looks like she is letting this shit go. All we need to do is wait, and it will all be mine. I'm not comfortable taking out a mother and a child. That's never been us."

"When the fuck did you turn into this person? Where is the take charge nigga I knew? All you do is complain about what you don't have, but I don't see you out here trying to get it. Now, let's go take what the fuck belongs to you."

I did all that to charge him up. As soon as we made it in the house, someone else came in behind us. We were about to make our move when Bruno pushed me back. Thinking he was punking the fuck out, I tried to get out of the room. Putting his finger up to his lips, I looked at him like he was crazy.

"It's not her, it's Spade. Shut the fuck up before we both die." How the fuck did he get out? Was he here to kill us or her? Did he see us come in? I had so many questions, but I had to wait to find out the answer. When he never came looking for us, I was able to calm my nerves. We watched him take Pebbles and her daughter. As soon as the coast was clear, Bruno stormed out and I followed behind him looking stupid. As soon as we got to the house, he beat my ass like I was a nigga that stole his pack.

Not even bothering to see if I was okay, he kicked me in my stomach on his way out of the door. Lying in my own blood, I cried like the weak bitch they thought I was.

Not being able to move, I laid in the same spot he left me in. By the time he came back, I was still right there looking pathetic and crying. I have no idea why he was so angry at me, but the shit had me plotting. Hearing the door open, I laid out on the floor pretending to be half dead. His ass was about to feel like shit for putting his hands on me. Feeling him stand over me, I smiled internally knowing he was about to kiss my ass. Hearing him walk off, my ass jumped up like a sissy doing a back hand stand. He had me fucked up.

"So, you not gone even check on me?" The nigga started laughing and poured him a drink.

"For what? A nigga didn't even hit you that hard for your ass to be trying to lay there and play dead. How the fuck you knocked out, but your wig still on tight as hell? I been beating bitches since 2005. I know how to hit a hoe." This nigga was sitting there bragging on having the proper beat a bitch etiquette.

"You could have still checked to see if I was okay. I don't even know why you pissed. I didn't fuck up, you chose not to do shit."

"That's why you got your ass whooped. What the fuck I was supposed to do? Spade is my nigga. He raised me and gave me his empire. It's not his fault he had a flawed ass bitch. If shit go like I think it will, his ass gone kill her and then I can take over the throne."

"What makes you think he not gone want his shit back? That nigga not in jail no more. He is not about to give you the empire. Your ass going to be the worker you always been."

"Bitch you were two Fridays away from selling pussy. Don't judge me. If that time comes, I will deal with it when it does. I'm not about to cross my man for no reason. He ain't been shit but good to me. Get your dumb ass in there and cook." Laughing, I walked towards the kitchen.

"Cook for what? You seem to like the scraps. I'm going to make me a sandwich and bring you the crumbs." You could tell he was pissed, but I was too. I'm trying to get our shit back to the way it was and his ass acting scared. If he content with how shit is, he could get the fuck out. I'm not about to play the fool for long.

"That's why your dumb ass sitting there with a knot on your shit now. You talk too fucking much. From now on, you let me do the thinking. It's obvious your dumb ass don't know shit about the street life. Keep it that way." Letting him thing what he wanted to, I started fixing dinner. If he didn't want to take out Pebbles, then I would. Even if that meant taking out Spade. Realizing I was missing some salad dressing, I grabbed some glasses and a purse and got ready to go to the store.

"I'll be back, I have to go get some ranch for the salad." The nigga didn't even look up.

"Don't do nothing stupid Halle. I promise I'll fuck you up. I been playing with your ass and trust me, you don't want this shit to get real." This nigga threatening me like he didn't just blacken my shit. My ass out here in the dark with sunglasses on. Fuck him, if he was too scared to do it, then I would. As soon as I walked up to my car, I saw someone standing there.

"Can you move, I'm trying to go somewhere?"

"I hope you're this feisty when it counts and not just some big mouth bitch that's all talk." Looking at this motherfucker like they were crazy, I was ready to pop off.

"Don't get fucked up. If I scream, my nigga will come air your ass out. Now, I'm asking you again to move."

"We can be of assistance to each other. You want the empire and I want Spade and Pebbles dead. We can help each other if you shut the fuck up long enough to listen." That shit caught my attention and I was ready to hear what this motherfucker had to say.

"My bad, but you don't just walk up on a bitch's shit without saying shit. This is Chicago and you can't trust a person that's just standing there. I'm interested in what you have to say, so what's up." Smiling, I listened as they told me the plan. The shit was brilliant, and I couldn't wait to get this shit going. Bruno didn't have a choice but to get on board with this shit. There was no way he wouldn't walk away with the empire if we followed the plan. We exchanged numbers and I opened my car door.

"I'll be in touch." Nodding my head, I got in my car and pulled off. This was a guaranteed way to get rid of both of them. Making my way to get the dressing, I decided not to tell Bruno until I got the call. No sense in telling his scary ass now. In due time, he will know everything.

CHAPTER SIXTEEN SHVONNE

Not giving a fuck about the money anymore, I gave Spade everything he needed to get his shit back. All I wanted was Jelly. Nothing else mattered. I'm a go getter, that means I will always get money. I've always been a born survivor, Bam made sure I would always be straight. The money was not worth my child's life.

If only I had listened to my best friend, it would have never come to this. I assumed I had time to fix it since his ass wasn't going anywhere. Or so I thought. Totally underestimating his reach, I slipped up. Now, me and my daughter could pay the price. All I could do is pray he would let me walk once he got all his shit back.

Hearing the door open, my ass was shaking like a crackhead needing a fix. This may have been the first time in my life I actually been scared. If it wasn't for Jelly, I would be okay with my fate. She only knew me, and she had already lost Tiana. This was something she would not understand. Spade walked over to me and I knew in my heart he wasn't about to let me go. Taking in his looks and his cologne, I wish I had done things differently. He would never know that I did have feelings for him, or that I loved him. No matter what I said, nothing would make him believe me. There was one more move I had to play though. If he was the man I thought he was, then it would work.

"Well Queen P, all my shit was there. It's good to know you don't lie about every fucking thing. Too bad you learned that shit a lil too late. You know, I loved you and I ain't never did that shit with nobody. My mama warned me against you, but I ignored her and continued to give you my all."

"Spade, listen. I know I fucked up." Raising his hand, he cut me off. There was nothing he wanted to hear from me. His ass just wanted to get it all out before he killed me.

"You had plenty of time to tell me how you felt. When I killed your nigga, that shit wasn't personal. I didn't know you or him. All I know is, that nigga was about to try me, and I couldn't allow that to happen. I won't apologize for choosing self-preservation. No matter what the fuck goes on, I will always choose me first. You came here with the intent to get me back. Every day, you plotted and schemed until you had me where you wanted me. The fake love, the fake tears, and the fake support. You could have kept that shit and stayed one hunnid. See, you think you are a savage, but a true savage looks someone in the eyes and take them out.

The niggas that killed my father, I went on their land and killed they ass. They knew why I was there and they knew it was do or die. Every nigga I killed in my life, I looked them in the eyes and did what I had to do. I'm a savage. Even savages get cocky and fuck up. Pebbles you aint shit but a bitch with a chip on her shoulder. On today, I'm about to knock that motherfucker clean off. I love you, but I love myself more." Grabbing his gun, he pointed it at my head. Praying my last card worked, I blurted it out.

"Jelly is your baby." His hand shook, but his face never changed. Keeping his gun on me, I could tell he was trying to read me.

"Pebbles, I don't believe shit you say. Your word doesn't carry any weight around here. Using a child as leverage is pathetic even for you."

"Did you even look at her? She is your fucking twin. Her name is Jalayia and we call her Jelly. Her last name is Spade. If you look in my purse, her social is in my wallet." Dropping the gun, I could tell this was fucking him up. Walking over to my belongings, he dumped the shit out of my purse. Looking in my wallet, I saw his expression change.

"How? You visited me, and you weren't pregnant. How the fuck is she mine?"

"When I came to see you, I covered it by wearing big clothes. You never paid attention because of the strict dress code the jail had. I didn't come visit you at the prison until after I had her. I'm sorry for not telling you, but what was I supposed to say? I'm sorry for setting you up, but you have a daughter. You can be her father from behind a glass."

"YOU SHOULD HAVE FUCKING TOLD ME." Punching the wall, he looked at me with fire in his eyes. You could tell he was conflicted. "My mother was out here, you took her son the least you could have done was let her see my child. Same selfish ass Shvonne where everything is always about you." When he walked over to me, I just knew he was about to kill me. Untying me, he walked away.

"I'm going to do a DNA and I'll bring her back. Spend as much time as you can because I'm coming back for my daughter. You're not fit to raise your arms let alone a child. Stupid ass bitch." Leaving me sitting there, I took a deep breath and got the fuck up out of there. I had to call an Uber, but I was just happy to be alive. As soon as I made it home, I showered and took my ass to bed. I'll deal with Spade's threats on tomorrow.

****

Either I was dreaming, or someone was in my house raping me. My pussy cat was throbbing, and it only does that when I get some head. I didn't feel none of that, but I damn sure knew what I dick felt like. Trying to jump up, I screamed when I was forced back down. I did my best to fight, but the person on top of me was entirely too strong. Tears welled up in my eyes as he slammed his dick in and out of me with force.

I've been through a lot in my life, but I have never been raped or molested. This was an all time low for me and I knew karma was beating my ass. Bending down, he bit me on my neck and that's when I smelled him. It was Spade. Not knowing how to feel about his actions, I let him have his way. He was torn between wanting me and needing to punish me. Knowing I deserved the pain I was feeling, I just laid there.

That was until my pussy started to betray me. It's like as soon as I realized it was him, she started dripping and the pain slowly subsided. Wanting him to know that I was willing, I tried to turn around. Slamming me down again, I knew he didn't want to look at me. Knowing all I could do was grind my hips against him, I threw it back on him as he continued to fuck my walls up.

"Spade, I'm about to cum." Instead of being excited, he slammed my face into the pillow and shoved it down as if he was trying to kill me.

"Shut the fuck up." Not being able to breathe and cumming at the same time, was causing me to have an intense reaction. Not being able to control it, my body started convulsing and it felt like I was about to die. I've never had that feeling before and it fucked my head up. Not able to move, Spade took advantage of that. Spitting on my asshole, I tried to find the energy to stop him from going in my ass.

Not being able to stop it, his ass worked his way in and I prayed my bowels stayed inside. His dick was big as hell, and he was already fucking me like he hated me. For some reason, he was

104

more gentle in my ass. The feeling had me gone in the head. Gripping my ass, he showed me how he felt with each stroke.

"Mmmmm shit. This feels so good Spade." As soon as he started beating my shit up, I knew I should have kept my mouth closed.

"I said shut the fuck up." Once he started ramming his dick inside of me, I couldn't say shit no way. His dick started jumping and I knew he was about to cum. His nasty ass slid out of my ass and went right back in my pussy. Biting into my shoulder, he came inside of me. Tears came out of my eyes since I wasn't allowed to speak. That bite hurt like a motherfucker.

Feeling him climb off me, I turned over and tried to talk to him. Seeing him get dressed hurt my heart. Spade was treating me like a hoe in the streets and I was ready to beat his ass. Knowing I was already on thin ice, I would just look for me a new place. Nigga wasn't about to walk in and out of my shit at will. He didn't speak one word to me as he walked out of my door. Crying, I screamed fuck Spade and took my ass to sleep.

CHAPTER SEVENTEEN SPADE

When I left out of Shvonne's house, I had no intentions on going back. So many emotions were going through my mind and I didn't know what to do with them. Anger was the only one I allowed to take over. How could this bitch keep a kid from me? Was she lying to stay alive? Would she have ever told me if I didn't have her held at gunpoint? I would never get the answer to that shit because her ass couldn't be trusted to tell the truth.

Jumping in my car, I drove to Walgreens. Grabbing DNA kit, I headed to my moms house. I had to see this lil girl for myself up close, but I still needed that shit in black in white. For the second time, my moms tried to tell me something and I didn't listen. My ass was so mad I had to focus to keep from swerving. Not wanting to get pulled over, I tried to get my mind right. Slowing down, I drove the rest of the way with a lot of shit on my mind.

As soon as I got to my moms house, I jumped out and ran to the door. Using my key, I rushed inside to find them. They were in the front room and it looked as if Jelly and my moms had been around each other for years. It was full of toys and they were dressed up having a tea party. It's never been a child here, so I know my moms had just bought it. The sight was awesome, and I instantly wanted Jelly to be mine.

"What's up y'all, can I play?" My moms looked up smiling as Jelly made me a place setting. Sitting at the little table, my tall ass looked like a fool. "Hey Jelly, I'm Spade." When she looked up at me, my heart stopped. No DNA would have to tell me I was the father. She was a splitting image of me as if I shot her out of my nut sack onto the delivery table. I didn't even realize I wasn't breathing until my moms started laughing.

"Told you. I don't know where you got this lil girl from, but she is yours all day long. This isn't the first time I saw her either. We were in Walmart one day and she was with this lady, but I had to stop and talk to her because she looked just like you. Shit broke my heart, but it made me feel closer to you. Then the lady took her and ran. I had no idea what was going on, but I know this baby is yours."

"Ma, that's Shvonne's daughter. She saying the baby is mine and I was coming to test her, but I don't have to. If I put a grill in her mouth, we would be twins. I went there to take her out and she told me this. How can I spade the mother of my daughter? If I don't hold up my end of the bargain, what will Valencia do? Ma, for the first time in my life, I'm lost on what move I should take." You could tell she was in deep thought.

"Son, you know I don't sugar coat shit. You know I don't like that girl and I hate what she did to my child. At the same time, I am a mother. I watched you hurt behind the lost of your father and he wasn't even a good one. All this baby knows is that girl, and if you

LOCKED DOWN BY HOOD LOVE 2

take that away from her, she will resent you when she is old enough. What's done in the dark always comes to the light. You won't be able to hide that from her forever.

I don't know this Valencia bitch or her motive, so I say your energy should be put into figuring out a way to deal with her. You know we are keen on family and I think you and her need to come to some kind of agreement about his baby. I know I will have to learn to like her mama if I want her in my life, and you are going to have to do the same. You have to find a way to deal with what she did to you and come to some type of terms."

"I told her I was going to get custody of the baby. She is unfit and don't deserve to raise my child. Selfish ass bitch." She slapped me so hard my jaw went numb for a few seconds.

"Don't you ever speak about this child's mother like that while she is sitting here. That's not how I raised you. Don't sit here and act like you didn't play a part in this. Yes, what she did was wrong and I don't like her ass. Son, at some point you are gone have to accept responsibility. Do you know how many families mourned behind some shit you and your father did? Some of the shit had no meaning behind it. Shit was all ego. Some stuff was valid. Either way, when you are in this lifestyle, you are bound to piss somebody off." What she said made perfect sense, but I was not ready to forgive her. Part of the reason was because I still loved her.

"Ma, she is going to spend the night with you and tomorrow I'm going to take her home. Me and Pebbles will tell her together. After that, I don't know what I'm going to do, but I have some business to handle tonight." You could tell she felt sorry for me and the predicament I was in.

"I trust you to make the right decision son. I have your back no matter what. Just remember this lil girl doesn't have anything to do with y'all's mess." Nodding, I got up and walked out. Jumping in my car, I found myself driving back to Shvonne's. I wasn't even trying to or thinking about it, but that's where my heart led me. When I got there, I watched her sleep for thirty minutes. Her ass crept up out from under the sheets and I my dick bricked up.

What would be the harm in fucking her? We already had history and shared a child. Plus, I was tired of that weak ass pussy Valencia was throwing. My dick was sore for a week after the first time we fucked, and I didn't use a condom. Damn dick had carpet burns. The way she fought me, I know she thought she was getting raped at first, then something gave me away. I don't know what it was, but I was glad she figured it out. I'm not a rapist and I would hate for anybody to feel like I took they shit. I'm too fly to take it from a bitch. I can admit that I was aggressive as fuck though. All the anger I felt came out with each stroke.

Not wanting to hear anymore lies or hear any more excuses, I got up and went downstairs. Whatever I was going to do, I needed

109

to do it based off my own thoughts and what I felt was best. I was done letting bitches cloud my judgement. What I was about to do though was get my money. Grabbing most of it, I left her some only because she had my daughter. Other than that, I would have left her ass dryer than Valencia's pussy.

Jumping back in my car, I stopped by the stash house to put my money up. Leaving back out, I headed to Valencia's house. I had some shit to get off my chest with that bitch. She had an entire file on Shvonne, how the fuck she didn't know about my child? Shit like this is why I don't trust her in this situation.

The only problem was me not knowing if she was the only person that knew about our arrangement. If I took her out, would someone know that it was me? I'm not even sure if I was about to back out of our agreement. It was too many thoughts running through my mind. Shvonne had my heart, but Pebbles fucked me over. Them bitches were one, but they were different. When she is Pebbles, you never knew what you were going to get. Could I trust that? Or would she try to take me out again?

Walking in the door, I couldn't worry about Shvonne. Right now, I had a bunch of doubts and didn't trust Valencia. She had some explaining to do, and I needed answers now.

CHAPTER EIGHTEEN VALENCIA

Following Pebbles was very informative. It was so many people after her, I didn't have to get Spade out to do my dirty work. All I had to do was let the chips fall where they may. She had crossed a lot of people and they wanted her ass gone. If Spade didn't fulfill his commitment, it was only a matter of time before someone else took her out. Spade would be dealt with and my son's death would still be avenged.

When I saw him kidnap her and the baby, I got excited. I screamed to myself, this is it. He's about to do it, but when he left, I snuck in and the bitch was still being held in his basement. About to take matters into my own hand, I saw him return. I got excited again, but this nigga left, and she came out right behind his ass. I followed her Uber to her house and sat outside.

Spade came back, but this time he left with bags after being in there for about an hour. I should have followed him, but I wanted to see if he handled his business. Of course, the bitch was still alive and I was starting to get pissed off. Why the fuck was he steady playing around with the shit? Heading to the kitchen, I grabbed a knife. Not wanting to be the one to do it, I threw all caution to the wind. She was sleep and I knew I could take her out with no questions asked.

Out of nowhere, I thought about it. I was sitting outside of her house in a government vehicle. What if her neighbors saw my car, or took down my plates? What if they saw me come in? I didn't take any precautions to hide who I was, and I knew this was not the time to take her ass out. Wiping the knife off, I slid out the door and got back in my car.

Heading home, I was pissed I almost jeopardized my career for some shit another nigga was supposed to do. The only reason he was free was because I thought we had a common enemy. His ass still in love and this bitch done got him three hundred years. Her pussy must be Ford tough, because she had his ass locked down. What kind of hold does she have on his ass, that he still ain't willing to take her out?

He had every opportunity to do it, and his ass keeps stalling. If he wasn't going to do it, then I would. Fuck him. His ass thinks he can play me, but he had another thing coming. Pulling up to the house, I parked and got out with an attitude. Walking inside, I slammed the shit out of the door, but to my surprise, he was standing there waiting on me like he was pissed. Before I could get my rant out, he grabbed me by my neck. My feet were dangling, and my breath was short.

"Did you know that Shvonne had a baby by me?" I noticed he called her Shvonne and not Pebbles this time. Yeah, his ass was back in her trap and didn't even know it.

"No." My lie came out in a whisper. Yeah, I knew about the baby, but fuck her and her mama. She took my son why would I give a fuck about her daughter's feelings?

"Don't lie to me Valencia. You have an entire file on her. How the fuck you didn't know she had my child?" Noticing I was turning colors and couldn't answer, he dropped me to the floor. After going through a coughing spell, I lied some more.

"I knew she had a baby, but how was I supposed to know she was yours? Did you know the baby was yours?" He got quiet, and I knew I had his ass. "Then how the fuck was I supposed to know? This girl got your mind tripping and you're caught the fuck up again. How the fuck you allow this bitch to trap you twice, yet you don't trust me, but I got you out of jail."

"Because I know her motives and what she is capable of. You, I don't trust what I can't see. I have no idea what you are willing to do or what you will do once I'm done. I don't trust you." Now, I was pissed.

"I don't give a fuck if you trust me or not. When I let you out of jail, we had a deal. You have yet to uphold your end. I did what I said. Now you have to do your part. You done let this girl get in your head. Okay, you're the father. Kill the bitch and get your daughter. We both know that's not it though, you don't want to kill her because you still love her."

"You think love go the fuck away? I bet you still love your lame ass husband. That shit don't mean nothing. I never stopped loving her ass, but that don't mean her ass can't get Spaded. All you bitches can get spaded at this point. I don't trust neither one of y'all, and I don't like my mind clouded. I told you a million times, let me do this shit on my time. I need to sort through my thoughts.

If the shit gets done, why the fuck do it matter? That's what bothers me, why are you so pressed for time? Your son not coming back, so what the fuck is the problem?" I couldn't tell him my supervisors gave me a month to lock his ass back up. There was no way I could tell him why I was pressed for time.

"I just think that if you take too long, you will get caught up in her lies again. The longer you wait, the easier it is for your feelings to come back. Not to mention, what the fuck have we been doing? You acting as if we don't have something going on." Even though I was reaching, and I knew we weren't on shit, I was pulling for straws. I didn't even like his ass, but it pissed me off when he fell out laughing.

"We don't have shit. You're a piece of pussy to fuck. I just came home, and I didn't want to be seen. I needed a nut, and you gave it to me. Barely, but I got it. Don't try to make this into something more. You knew what the fuck this was."

"Fuck you Spade. If we ain't shit, then you can keep that tired ass dick. I'm not pressed for a nut. Do what I got you out for, and we can go our separate ways."

"You wish this dick was tired. My mans was probably tired of being scratched the fuck up from your sand dust ass pussy. Fuck out of here with the dumb shit. You don't run me. It will be done when I say it will be done." Walking off, he left me standing there fuming. Oh, it was going to be done whether he did it or not. When his ass got locked back up, I won't feel an ounce of regret. Fuck Spade.

Grabbing my phone, I needed to make a few calls to set some shit in motion. I needed to handle Pebbles, because it was obvious Spade's ass wasn't going to do it. Fuck him and that bitch.

CHAPTER NINTEEN SHVONNE

Waking up, my pussy was still thumping from the bruising Spade put on my shit. Running to the bathroom, I damn near had to grab my ass cheeks. As soon as I sat on the toilet, shit flew out and the shit hurt like hell. Scooting up, I left one of the cheeks on the toilet seat and the other one I had tooted in the air. I don't know if it was going to work, but I needed to do something. Once I was done, I patted my ass because I couldn't wipe. Niggas always wanted to fuck you in the ass, but they didn't know the next day a bitch be fighting to keep her bowels in.

Jumping in the shower, I got my hygiene together. My ass was hurting, but the water soothed it. Spade knew damn well his dick was too big to be going in somebody booty hole. It's a booty hole nigga. Walking damn near bowlegged, I grabbed a towel and walked into my room. Spade was sitting on my bed, and I almost lost my bowels again. My damn muscles were loose as a goose and I prayed I didn't shit on this floor in front of him.

"Jelly is in her room. Go get her dressed and meet me at my moms. We need to explain to her who I am, and I would like to take her somewhere. I know she may not be comfortable with me yet, so you can come this time. Besides, you need all the time you can get with her." I was over this nigga's attitude, but I was trying to be compassionate to his feelings. He was trying me though.

"I have to go make arrangements for Tiana. Since she was a foster kid, nobody will come and handle it. I think I'm going to cremate her like I did Bam. I'm sure you don't care, but I have to do it. That was my best friend. Fighting back tears, I didn't want to break down and shit on myself because I was doing the ugly cry.

"Why wouldn't I care? The reason I'm so pissed off is because of how I feel about your ass. I'm not you." How the fuck he gone say he care, but he killed her?

"If you cared, you wouldn't have taken her from me." The nigga looked at me all weird like and even though I tried not to, the tears fell.

"You said that shit the other night and I thought you were talking out of your ass to keep me from killing you. Why the fuck would I kill Tiana? You're the only person I have beef with Shvonne." Now I was confused.

"Wait, if you didn't kill her, then who did?" He shrugged his shoulders, but I knew he wasn't lying. That means, someone else out there was after me and Jelly still wasn't safe. Not wanting to ask Spade for help, I kept quiet. If he was thinking the same thing as me, he didn't say a word.

"I'll be at my moms waiting." Without a second thought, he left out. He says he loves me, but the Spade I knew wouldn't have walked off while I was crying. His ass would have moved mountains to figure out who the fuck was after me. It's cool though, fuck

117

Spade. I was trying to go about this the right way, but if a bitch is what he wanted, then a bitch is what he would get.

Throwing my clothes on, I made sure I looked good and I headed to Jelly's room. She was playing with her new toys I'm sure Ms. Janice had gotten her. I wish I didn't have to interrupt her, but I was about to take her to Spade, tell her who he is, and go to the hospital. He can go out with her by his damn self. If he thinks I'm going to let him get custody of my baby, he had another thing coming.

"Come on Jelly, you have to take a bath and wash up."

"Play mommy."

"No, bath. You can play later." She was sad, but she got up and did what I asked her to do. After getting her together, I made sure I had everything and walked out. As soon as I made it to the porch, Bruno was standing there with a gun pointed at me. My ass just wanted to pass out, I could not catch a fucking break.

"My daughter is right here, I suggest we talk later. Whatever it is you want, I'm sure we can work it out."

"It's too late for all that bitch. You want me to beg for something that was given to me? Huh bitch? Spade gave that shit to me, but you wanted it all. All you had to do was give me what was rightfully mine, now I'm going to take it." Closing my eyes, for what seemed like the umpteenth time, I prayed for my soul. Feeling something wet hit my face, I opened them fast as hell. Spade was running up the driveway firing away. He told me he was leaving. I don't know what made him come back, but I was happy as fuck that he did.

"Why the fuck is Bruno trying to take you out Shvonne? This is why I'm taking Jelly from your ass. You have too many people after you and she has witnessed too much already." This nigga thought he could just come in and take the fuck over. Nigga been a daddy twenty seconds and thinks he in charge.

"Don't come for my motherhood. You the one that told this nigga he can have the empire when you knew I was running it. He felt the shit was his and was trying to take it. Fuck him." Kicking Bruno in his bleeding head, I walked off. "Call the fucking clean up crew. I'll meet you at your mother's house. If the bitch get out of line, you gone need one for her too. I'm sick of your fucking family." He laughed, but I was dead ass serious. This shit was starting to get out of hand. It seems like everyone that has had any damn problem with me was trying to take me out. I still don't know who the fuck killed Tiana. I know Jelly isn't safe, but she is mine. I will move the fuck away before I let Spade take her from me. Strapping her in, I jumped in the car and drove off burning rubber. I don't drive fast with Jelly in the car, but I wanted to do that shit for the effect. That nigga needed to know I was pissed off.

I swear I wasn't in the mood for his mama's shit, but I knew if I didn't come me and Spade would be at it. Getting out, I grabbed

Jelly and walked to the door. Taking a deep breath, I put on a smile trying to pretend I was happy to see her ass. Jelly's ass was too excited when she opened the door.

"Yayyyy." Ms. Janice grabbed her and hugged her like it's been days.

"You just left me and you're back already. You miss me Jelly bean?" No the fuck she wasn't about to change her name.

"It's just Jelly. How are you Ms. Janice?" The bitch gave me a head nod. I started to kick her in her knee caps. I don't care how good an old bitch looked, if you wanted to remind them of their age, kick them in them knees. Bet they remember.

"Come on Jelly. Let's go make some cookies. You want to help me bake some cookies baby?" Jelly was beaming with joy.

"Yes." I don't know why, but I felt a certain kind of way. All this time she has been just mine. Now I have to share her, and I really didn't want to. That was half the reason I never wanted to tell her or Spade that she existed. I knew they would want her just as much. To see her want someone else as much as me, or happy to see the next motherfucker made me feel a way.

Sitting down on the couch, I waited for Spade to bring his ugly ass here. He was gone have to get his mama in check. Yeah, he was the father, but his mama wasn't about to be changing names and running shit. Speaking of running, I jumped up grabbing my ass cheeks looking for a bathroom. I swear I hate that nigga Spade.

CHAPTER TWENTY HALLE

After meeting up with my contact person that day, I rushed home hoping Bruno would be willing to do the plan. It sounded like a good one to me, but his ass was a flunky. He actually gave a fuck about Spade and that was going to pose as a problem. I needed him to get on board. When I walked in the house, he was sitting there drinking. I gave that nigga my best motivational speech ever.

"Baby get your ass up and get your shit together. I got the perfect plan and even you can't turn this shit down. Now, I know you said you don't want to do this, but I know you got this."

"Halle, would you stop it with this shit. Damn, I think you're more obsessed with Pebbles than I am. Who the fuck got played? Me or you? If you want to do something with that brain of yours, you can always give me some head. Fuck out of here." This nigga was content on being a drunk lying on the couch.

"Bae, I get that. I just know you're better than this. I was a part of the crew and I saw how you ran that shit. The niggas respected you and they listened. You knew how to talk to them and for that, they respected you. Baby everything about you says King. Don't you sit and wonder what it would be like to be on top of the world. King Bruno, that shit has a ring to it. You don't deserve to be anybody's second hand. Even when Spade got locked up, he should have put you in charge.

They know you were a beast, that's why they kept you second in command. He still didn't respect you enough to let you run it while he was away. That's because he knew you would take that shit from him." You could see him thinking over what I said. He was buying that shit. "They didn't respect you like you thought they did."

"I didn't do what I did for respect. I'm a loyal nigga and I'm going to do my job. If they didn't appreciate that shit, that's on they ass. I still don't see what this has to do with Pebbles." Smiling, I sat down across from him.

"It has everything to do with her. If you kill Pebbles and Spade her, you won't have to take Spade out. They gone lock his ass back up. That way, he never has to know you crossed his ass. It's a foolproof plan. He is going to put you in charge once they gone anyway. You just moving the pieces to get to the front. She did the same thing to that nigga, it's only right she goes out the same way. You can be the one that take her down. Do you know how big that is? Motherfuckers would fear you off that alone."

"If I do this, how do we get them alone? Spade been around her lately. That nigga not gone sit by and let me kill that bitch, even if he is pissed at her ass." I felt like I should be the nigga in charge if I had to do all this. Damn. Common sense should kick in somewhere.

"We were already following her. We sit and wait. When he leaves, you kill her ass and leave the trademark. We sit in the car and wait for him to come back and then call the police. He will never know you were involved in any way."

"When you wanna do it?"

"In a couple of days. Make sure it's early to. That way, we not confused on who is who. That bitch got a lot of people after her, we don't want to make any mistakes."

"I love when you get street Halle. Come give me some of that pussy. Daddy dick hard as a motherfucker." Rolling my eyes, I walked away.

"You got me fucked up. When you show me you daddy by completing this, I'll let you do whatever you want to this pussy."

Now here we were, sitting outside of Pebble's house. Just like I thought, Spade's ass was in there and left back out. As soon as he pulled off, I turned to Bruno. It was now or never.

"Come on daddy, you got this. Go take that bitch out and get what's yours." Leaning over, he kissed me, and I gave him all the tongue. Just the thought of what he was about to do turned me on. Jumping out of the car, he waited outside of her house. Smiling, I was feeling really good about the shit. When Pebbles walked out, she looked like she saw death waiting on the porch.

Out of nowhere, I saw Bruno's head explode. Looking over, Spade was coming full force back towards the house. Trying not to draw attention to myself, I drove off slow as hell. The tears came down hard as hell. This bitch was like a fucking dark cloud over my life. How the fuck does she keep coming out on top, but everyone else around her was going through hell or dying like they had the fucking plague?

This bitch had to have some kind of guardian angel watching over her. The shit hurt. Pebbles gets to step on everyone else, while she continues to live high and mighty. Fuck. Fuck. Fuck. I can't believe my man is gone. My ass had to pull over I was crying so hard. Not knowing what else to do, I picked up my phone.

"They killed him. They killed Bruno. I hate that fucking bitch. What am I going to do now?"

"First, you're going to get your shit together. Stop crying and listen. I have a fucking plan. You have to avenge Bruno, but you're going to need to man the fuck up." Listening, I prayed this shit worked. I was sick of this bitch. Too scared to go back to the house, I drove to a hotel and got a room.

Everything came crashing down as soon as I walked in the door. This shit was all my fault; I'm the one that pushed him to do the shit. He was trying to let the shit go, but I was too caught up on revenge. I should have listened to him, and he would still be here. If shit hadn't gotten so bad with us, I wouldn't have pushed him so hard. I just wanted things to go back to the way they were.

Needing someone else to blame in order to feel good about myself, I shifted that shit right back to Pebbles. If she would have given him his shit when he came home, none of this would have happened. Instead, she acted like he was nothing and treated me like shit. You can't treat people like that and not expect shit to come back on you.

Somehow, someway, she always walked away untouched. I was sick of her ass, and it was time for me to do what everyone else was scared to do. It was time for that bitch to go. She was about to meet her match; I bet that bitch wouldn't think I was weak anymore. Picking up the phone, I called my mama. She answered on the first ring.

"Hey ma, Bruno is dead and it's all that bitch's fault. I know you are going to tell me to leave it alone; I just wanted you to know if anything happens to me, I didn't go out like somebody's bitch."

"You sound bout stupid as fuck. Losing your life is going out like a bitch. If you had left it alone when I told you to, none of this shit would have happened. You want to blame everybody else, but this shit falls on you. Grow up. So what, she didn't want to be your friend anymore. She didn't want you to work with her. Oh fucking well. Do you realize how crazy that sounds?" I don't know what made me call her, maybe it was the grief clouding my judgment.

"Ma, I didn't call for permission. You sit your ass there being a door mat for every nigga that comes into your life. All you do is sit there smoking squares and cry when they leave. What the fuck do you know?" Hanging up the phone, I went over my next move in my head. Fuck my mama and fuck Pebbles. She couldn't keep getting away with this shit.

CHAPTER TWENTY-ONE SPADE

Shit was getting out of hand, and I had no idea who all this girl done pissed off. Motherfuckers were coming out like roaches in the dark and she didn't see shit wrong with it. Even though I just found out I was a father, I didn't want to lose her. The rate Shvonne was going, shit was going to get worse before it got better.

Here I was conflicted about killing her ass, and now I'm saving her. When I saw it, shit came second nature. I didn't even think about it. As soon as I saw she was in trouble, I fired off. If I had left like I was supposed to, I wouldn't have been there to pop that nigga Bruno. When I left out, I felt bad for leaving her in there crying.

My dumb ass was sitting in the car trying not to get sucked back in. She thought I had killed Tiana, but it wasn't me. Knowing somebody else was after her, didn't sit right with me. Niggas didn't know she played me, and that means they thought shit was sweet. Motherfuckers knew not to come after what was mine. That told me, it was a nigga out here who was bold enough to try me. Sitting there wondering if I should go back in and apologize, I saw Bruno walking up. I didn't think he was there to kill Pebbles, my ass thought she was fucking him behind my back. Pulling my gun out, I twisted on my silencer and got ready to kill both of their asses.

When I saw him pull his gun, all I wanted to do was save her. Without hesitation, I jumped out of my car and started blasting. Not trying to give him the chance to hit her, I gave him a head shot as soon as I aimed. You could tell Shvonne was scared, but as soon as I opened my mouth, the old Pebbles returned. That's the person I fell in love with. That spark is what made her different from everyone else.

Laughing, I called the clean up crew since I was no longer in hiding. The niggas were shocked to hear from me. I'm guessing they heard how much time I got and they went crazy when they heard my voice.

"Somebody gotta be playing a joke on me right now. My nigga King Spade in the booty house trying not to drop the soap. Ain't no way he on my line asking for a clean up." Beano was talking shit, but I can see why they would be confused.

"You know damn well they can't keep a nigga like me down. On King Leel, I would have shot my way up out that bitch before I did three hundred." He laughed, but he knew I was talking shit.

"Shoot them with what nigga? Your nut. Where you want this crew at before your ass be back up in that bitch?"

"They can try, but a nigga like me never going up in that bitch again. Y'all gone be around here singing day after day. My ass going out like Cleo. Fuck you talking about. Bring your ass on, I got some shit to do. I'm texting the address." Hanging up the phone, I waited until they got there.

Shit went smooth and easy. Even though everything was cleaned up, I didn't feel comfortable with them coming back here. It seemed like every day something else was popping off with her. This was the reason I wanted to get my daughter. If this was the life she wanted to live, she could do that shit by herself. Not with a fucking Spade.

Pulling up to my mom's house, I walked in the house and looked around for my baby. I couldn't get enough of her. She looked so much like me the shit was creepy. Her and my moms was in the kitchen, while Pebbles sat on the couch looking like somebody stole her fucking bike.

"Fuck wrong with you? Same ol Pebbles mad at the fucking world."

"Fuck you Spade. Y'all trying to take my baby and turn her against me. They in there making cookies and shit and didn't ask me if I wanted a fucking morsel. Fuck y'all." I couldn't help but laugh, she was jealous, but she kept my baby from me for almost two years.

"Well, get used to the shit, because you ain't got long with my seed. You can visit her, and I'm not gone keep you away from her. It's just not safe for her to be with you. Motherfuckers trying to kill your ass every day." She jumped up and ran in the kitchen.

Damn near dragging Jelly to the front room, I was pissed how she was handling her.

"Jelly, I want you to meet somebody. This your father Jaleel. Can you say daddy?"

"Daddy."

"That's right, this is your daddy and that is your granny." Moms got mad as hell.

"Jelly don't listen to her. I already told you to call me glammy. Ain't that right baby?"

"Jelly loves Glammy." We all laughed.

"Oh, you don't have no love for your daddy? Come give me a hug." When she ran to me, that was the greatest feeling in the world. I should have been there from the beginning and that alone had me pissed again.

"Okay, y'all got that out of the way. Me and Jelly about to get up out of here. I mean, I need to spend all the time I can with her. Right? Come on Jelly." This bitch was about to piss me off, and she knew what the fuck she was doing.

"When you done at the hospital, go back to my house. Your shit ain't safe. I'm not staying there, so you will be good there. Find you a new spot quick though, I don't trust you in my shit." Rolling her eyes, she walked out of the house. Looking at my mom's face, I knew I was about to hear her shit.

"Why the fuck you keep doing that girl like that? I don't even like her ass, but even I know your ass is wrong. The girl ain't shit, we already know that, but she trying. Let the ain't shit bitch make up for what the fuck she did. Damn. You so damn stubborn, I don't know where you get that shit from." Looking at her like she lost her mind, I couldn't do shit but laugh.

"I get the shit from you. If she trying, why the fuck you not trying to let that shit go? You mad at her like she did something to your ass. Just like I'm still pissed, you are too. How the fuck do I let it go when I can't trust her ass?"

"I can't tell you what to do, but for once in your life, listen to your mama. Let that shit go." Thinking over what she said, I dozed off. I didn't even know I was sleep until I heard a gun cock in my face. I could hear that shit if I was under water. Opening my eyes, my blood started boiling when I saw it was Pebbles. This was why I couldn't trust her ass, I never knew if she was going to try and take me out. This bitch had shit twisted though. Not cracking a smile, I looked her dead in her eyes.

"You better be about to kill me bitch. Show me how tough you are. Not no snake shit getting a nigga locked up. Right here in my face, man the fuck up." You could see her wavering and I knew she didn't really want to kill me. Making my move, I pulled my gun on her. Standing up, we were facing off. Gun pointed at each other, it was about to be some shit blazing in this motherfucker.

"What the fuck is wrong with y'all? Both of you motherfuckers have lost it. This is my house and I'm not for the shit. You have a daughter and you need to learn how to co-exist together. Get your fucking shit together. Where the fuck is Jelly?"

"You think I'm stupid? I see y'all motherfuckers think I'm stupid. As soon as you said you were going to take my baby, somebody snatched her ass. I will kill both of you bitches." Before I knew it, moms had slapped the shit out of Pebbles.

"Get your disrespectful ass out of my house, before I drag your ass. All this time, I've been talking his ass out of killing you because of my grandbaby, but your bitch ass gone stand in my house and accuse me of some shit, then threaten me. Do you know who the fuck you dealing with? You say you Queen P, but I'm the original Queen around this bitch. I paid my fucking dues and no new ass bitch wearing a training bra is going to act like I didn't. I don't know what the fuck is going on with you two, but you better fucking fix it and go find my fucking baby. Or it's me that is going to kill one of you motherfuckers. Simple ass bitches." Lowering my gun, I looked over at Shvonne.

"Tell me exactly what the fuck happened. Don't leave shit out. If I find out you playing with me, I will kill you dead. Ain't no more of that dumb ass shit. Now start from the fucking beginning."

CHAPTER TWENTY-TWO SHVONNE

After storming out of Ms. Janice's house, I headed to the hospital to make arrangements for Tiana. Not wanting to leave her there like nobody cared, I had to go and get her. Putting in for her to be cremated, I was going to give her the same send off like I did Bam. She deserved to be free. Nobody would be at the funeral anyway. After I was done with everything, I left and headed to my house.

If I was going to be staying at Spade's house, me and Jelly were going to need some things. Walking into my house, I had that same feeling the night that Spade kidnapped my ass. Looking around, I didn't see anybody. Holding Jelly close, I walked around the house. Nobody was in there and I laughed at me being paranoid.

These motherfuckers had my head all fucked up. It seemed like somebody was after my ass every way I turned. Finally feeling at ease, I went in my room and grabbed some stuff. Heading into Jelly's room, I grabbed her some shit as well. Once we were done, we went to where I had my money stashed. When I lifted the floor, most of it was gone. I didn't know Spade had actually taken it, but I was glad he left some for me.

After I had everything, we walked out the door. Strapping Jelly in, I walked around to get in my car only to be met by a gun.

Whoever it was, they were wearing a mask. Not knowing what they wanted, I waited for them to say something. They never did, walking around the car, they grabbed Jelly and took off.

Chasing behind them, I tried my best to get my baby. They started shooting at me and it was nothing I could do. Dropping to the ground, all the fuck I could do was cry. The one person I tried to protect, was now gone. Out of nowhere, Spade's words hit me. Oh he had me fucked up right quick. Making sure my gun was loaded, I headed back over to Ms. Janice's house. If that nigga wanted a war, he could get one.

What I didn't expect was to get the shit slapped out of me by his mama. I let the shit slide because I did disrespect the fuck out of her in her house. At the end of the day, I wanted my daughter and I didn't care what came out of my mouth. Hearing them say they didn't have her, panic set in. This nigga was yelling in my face for me to tell him what happened. I could barely breathe, but knowing we needed to find her, I tried to get it out.

"Pebbles, who the fuck did you cross? In all my years of being in charge, I never had a motherfucker come at me like this. What was your ass out here doing?" That was the crazy part, I had no idea who the fuck was after me.

"When they started coming at me, I don't know what happened. I assumed it was you sending your people at me to get me back. If I knew what the fuck was going on, I would have already handled the shit. You think you're the only savage out here? When you were gone, I held this shit down. They feared me. Hell, they were probably more scared of me than you. None of this shit started happening until you brought your ass home. Wait. How the fuck did you get out anyway?" You could see the wheels turning in his head. The nigga was sexy as hell when he was in boss mode.

"I know who has her." Ready to go lay down whoever the fuck it was, I instantly got war ready. Before he could answer, my phone rung. Spade motioned for me to put it on speaker.

"Who is this?"

"How does it feel to lose the one thing you cared about?" Listening intently, I realized I knew the voice.

"Halle?"

"The one and fucking only. You treated me like shit, took Bruno's empire, and then you and that bitch ass nigga killed him. Now I have your lil girl. What will you do to get her back? That's if I don't feel like avenging Bruno thru your seed. I wonder what it would sound like if I took a bat to her fucking skull." My body began shaking and I could no longer talk. I was so angry, I could kill this bitch through the phone. Spade, spoke up to try and talk to her.

"How much do you want Halle? I'm sure you're not a dumb person. If you touch my daughter, there isn't a place on this earth you can hide from me. Knowing that you can't get away from me, let's be reasonable. Take the money and give me my daughter."

This bitch did a psycho ass laugh and it scared me. The bitch sounded unhinged.

"I don't want your fucking money. You think that shit means something to me. Once this shit is over with, I know my life is over. But I won't be the only one to go. If you want your daughter back, you have to give me something just as important." We were all confused.

"What is that?" Spade was looking crazed, while Ms. Janice cried. My ass was still shaking like a stripper.

"I want Pebbles. She comes alone, and I will tell you where you can get your daughter from." Everybody looked at me like wellll, somebody had to go. I felt like they kicked me the fuck off the top bunk.

"Deal, but you better know I don't play games. You getting what you want, give me my baby."

"I'll text you the address to send the bitch. After I have her in my custody, I'll text you where to get your daughter." Hanging up the phone, I knew that shit wasn't about to go that simple. This hoe had something up her sleeve and it was about to get ugly. Thinking it over, I came up with a plan and I prayed it worked.

"Ma, me and you are going to follow Pebbles. Once I get the address of Jelly, you go get her and I'll save Pebbles, again." The nigga said it like I was a burden. Yeah, he has been saving me, but he ain't have to say the shit like that.

"Anything for my daughter, even if that means sacrificing my life. You just make sure you get her back. Don't let that bitch win."

"You know I'm not about to let her do shit to you. If anybody gone lay your ass out, it's going to be me. I'm the only one with a legitimate excuse to kill your ass. I don't trust what she is saying, so everybody need to be willing to improvise. We don't know what we are walking into, and I have no idea if someone else is helping her. Ma, make sure you're strapped."

"Nigga, I stay locked and loaded. Don't play with me. Y'all better meet me back at this house in an hour, or I'm coming in that bitch shooting." Even though nothing was funny about this situation, I laughed my ass off at Ms. Janice. I've heard stories about her from Spade, but it seems weird to see her in that way. There wasn't an ounce of fear in her eyes and I admired that. When I got her age, I wanted motherfuckers to still fear me.

"Make sure you keep your phone on ma just in case. Pebbles, are you ready? The text just came through." We all got in separate cars and drove to our destination. My nerves were shot, but I had to get Jelly back. No matter the cost. When I pulled up, I had a feeling that was the last time I would see Spade. I never got to tell him that I do love him. Even though he may not have believed me, I wish I had gotten the chance to get that off my chest. At least I knew that Jelly would be in good hands with him and his mom. I could finally see Bam again. Walking into the

address given, I was walking into my fate.

CHAPTER TWENTY-THREE SPADE

This shit was crazy, and I had no idea what was going on anymore. Everything was all over the place and it seemed like everyone wanted a piece of Pebbles. Had she listened to me, and given the shit to Bruno, none of this would have happened. She was too busy trying to be Queen P, that she bit off more than she could chew. Now we out here trying to get my daughter back from a bitch that never mattered to begin with.

Sitting in the car, I could only imagine what the hell Jelly was thinking. That baby has witnessed more in these past few weeks, than some grown ass men have seen. Luckily, she was only a baby and would not remember shit. She had to be alright, I haven't gotten any time. I just found out about her, and now this bitch Halle had her. It's been so much going on, I forgot all about Valencia. When her number came across my screen, I started not to answer.

"Where the fuck are you Jaleel? I'm assuming you still chasing up behind that bitch. You're not going learn that bitch is toxic. All she wants to do is take and take until there is nothing left. Your ass to blind to see it, and when you do it will be too late." I could see why her husband left. All she does is fucking nag and complain. Everything that comes out of her mouth is fucking annoying.

"The way you talk shit you would think you got some good ass pussy. What the fuck do you want Valencia? No, I haven't done it yet. Before you ask, and I'm kind of in the middle of something." You could hear the bitch smack her lips.

"Where are you Jaleel? I can come to you so we can talk. I hate how the shit ended between us, and at the end of the day, we still have business to discuss." Not wanting her to know my whereabouts, I lied.

"I'm handling some shit for my moms. Shit shouldn't take that long. We good though. Shit will be done soon." She got quiet for a minute.

"Why the fuck do you treat me like I did something to you? All the fuck I ever did was help your ass. You're free because of me and you treat me like I'm the one that crossed you. Just let me come talk to you face to face. We can talk it out." This bitch was getting on my fucking nerves. In that moment, I made up my mind. I would have to take her out. I wasn't about to let her dictate my actions because she had an issue with Shvonne.

"Look, shit ain't working out. I'm good. You take care of yourself and I hope you are able to come to terms with your son's death, but if you come near my baby mama your ass is dead. Take your L and move the fuck around." Hanging up the phone, I looked and saw I missed the text from Halle. Calling my moms, I hope I wasn't too late.

"I just got the text. You need to get to Hazel Crest. It's a warehouse out that way. I'm going to text you the exact address. Be careful and make sure you get my baby. Call me when you're done."

"Nigga don't talk to me like I'm not from the same streets as you. I'm too old to be out here in gun wars fucking around with y'all shit. Get that girl so this shit can be over. You about to pay me out the ass for this shit."

"Ma, go handle your business. I need to get in here to Pebbles. Make sure you check in. I'll talk to you in a minute."

"Okay, be safe son." Hanging up the phone, I made my way around the back of the house she was in. It was quiet, and I couldn't tell where they were. Not wanting to just bust in, I had to figure out what part of the house they were in. Looking in the back window, all I saw was empty rooms. Having to take a chance, I eased in the door. Walking as light as I could, I was trying to make sure I didn't make any noise.

After tip toeing around the house, I didn't see them. Realizing there was a basement, I knew that was a tricky situation. She would see me coming and be able to shoot my ass in the leg. Pulling the door open, I walked down the stairs slowly. You could hear yelling, and I hoped their back was to me. When I made it to the bottom of the stairs, I cringed at the sight before me. Pebbles was fucked up bad and I knew I had to get her out of there soon.

She was beating her with the gun and as I got closer, I realized she spaded her while she was still conscience. This bitch was going to frame me for the murder. Raising my hand back to the Mississippi, I cold cocked that bitch over her head. She instantly dropped.

"Shvonne, can you hear me? Baby, wake up. I have to get you out of here." She was groggy, but I can see she was alive. My heart rate was able to slow down, but I was pissed the fuck off.

"Do you have Jelly? Please tell me you have Jelly." Knowing Hazel Crest wasn't around the corner, there was no way she was there yet. It would be a minute.

"I'm waiting to hear from my mama. She has to go way out baby. I'm sure Jelly is okay. Right now, we have to handle this bitch. Are you up to it, or do I need to take you to the hospital right away? If Jelly is at the other house, somebody is helping her. We need to find out who." I hated keeping her here while she was bleeding and fucked up, but I needed to get answers from this bitch before it was too late. Shvonne was a fighter, all I needed was five minutes and we could get out of here.

"Do what you need to. I'll be okay. I have to make sure Jelly is straight." Since she was knocked out cold, I untied Shvonne and headed upstairs to look for some shit I could use. Seeing a lighter, I searched around for some alcohol. This shit would have to work. Walking back to the basement, I put her in the same chair she had my girl in. After tying her up, I needed the bitch to wake up and

LOCKED DOWN BY HOOD LOVE 2

LATOYA NICOLE

answer some questions. Pouring the alcohol on her, I set her ass on fire. That heat woke her up instantly. Putting the fire out, I sat down in front of her. Seeing she had no way out and Pebbles loose, the punk bitch started crying.

"It's all her fault. The bitch had to get cocky and she got Bruno killed. She deserves everything she gets." Halle started laughing hysterically again, and that let me know this shit wasn't over.

"You're going to burn alive and she is going to watch. All your hatred and you are going to die knowing she won. It's only one way to save your life. Tell me who is helping you."

"Fuck her. The only thing I hate is that I won't get to see you die stupid bitch." This bitch was tougher than I thought she was. Knowing I had to break her, I poured the alcohol over her head.

"I don't think you realize how long it takes for someone to burn to death. The smell of your flesh burning is enough to drive a person insane. You are going to tell me if you want to live." When she didn't say anything, I walked over to her with the lighter. She screamed out a name and I shook my head in disgust. Setting the bitch on fire, I grabbed Pebbles and got the fuck out of there.

CHAPTER TWENTY FOUR VALENCIA

This nigga thought I was stupid, but he had another thing coming. He thought I was going to take this shit lying down. Watching him and that bitch reunite while he played the fuck out of me. That shit wasn't happening no matter what he thought. Getting out of my car, I dragged Jelly by her hair. Taking her inside of Pebbles' house, I put her in the basement and locked her in the room.

Jumping back in my car, I headed towards Hazel Crest. I was smarter than he gave me credit for. Texting the address to Halle, I waited for a little while and called Spade. At first, the nigga still tried to play me like I was a dumb bitch. Out of nowhere, he let my ass down and didn't give a fuck about it.

Even though I made preparations to handle him if he betrayed me, I was still shocked he would do me like this. That nigga would be rotting in jail if it wasn't for me. All I wanted him to do was take out the bitch that set his ass up and he couldn't even do that. You would think he would have been jumping for joy to take that bitch out. Instead, his ass come home and fall for her ass again. What kind of shit was that?

My eye started twitching I was so mad. It's okay though. Not only would I be able to avenge my son, but I would be able to avenge myself. If Halle did everything like she was supposed to, then things will work out perfectly. If that bitch was incompetent, I had a back up plan for that as well.

Following Spade around, I kept seeing the same car following Pebbles as well. Deciding to follow them one day to see where they went, I waited outside for one of them to come out. Halle walked out looking pissed off. I gave her an offer she couldn't refuse. Telling her all about the plan to take Pebbles out and frame Spade, she was all for it. Until Bruno got his dumb ass killed.

Knowing a parent would do anything for their child, I convinced her to take the baby. Pebbles would turn herself in and trade herself for the child. Knowing how Spade felt about her, I knew he would go looking. His ass is going to kill the fuck out of Halle and I didn't give a fuck. She was a casualty of war. Most people snitch under pressure, so I'm sure she will give my name. When he came looking for her, I'm going to kill him. The police will think it's a murder suicide and case would be closed. Especially since they want that nigga locked up anyway. I had the shit mapped out.

Getting out of the burner car I had, I walked in the warehouse. Hiding behind the door, I stood there waiting until he came in. It took him an hour to get there, but the adrenaline kept me alert. As soon as the door opened, I stepped around and hit him over the head. Looking down, I realized it was his mama and got pissed. He was fucking up the plan and I had to think of something else.

Making sure she wouldn't wake up on me, I hit her over the head five more times to make sure she was good and sleep. Dragging her to the car, I placed her inside and drove back to Pebbles' house. He would never look for them there and it was the perfect hiding spot. When I pulled up, I made sure nobody was around and dragged her old ass in the house. Locking her in the room with their daughter, I left out as quickly as I came in He would be calling me shortly and I needed to come up with a plan.

Everything was starting to fall a part and I needed to make sure he was framed for the shit, or making it look like he killed his self. Hearing my phone ring, I had no idea what to say, but I was going to wing it.

"Now you want to talk huh. Well, I'm busy and I don't have shit to say to you." I knew that would piss him off, but I was trying to buy some time.

"Bitch stop playing with me. Where the fuck is my baby? Don't make this harder than it has to be. You know the ending to this story, I don't even know why you want to fuck with me." Nigga was mad as hell. I almost clutched my pearls.

"You real cocky for a nigga that has no cards to deal. Tell me something, if I give them to you, what are you going to give me?"

"What the fuck you mean them?" I'm sure in that moment he was realizing how he fucked up.

"Your daughter and your mama. How bad do you want them back?" I had to hold in my laugh when I heard him punching something.

"You already killed Shvonne, what more do you want? You got what you wanted. WHAT THE FUCK DO YOU WANT?" Hearing him say Pebbles was dead made my pussy wet. That was the best news I heard all fucking year. "All I want is my baby girl."

"Fuck you, I'm not done with you yet. Your ass thought you could play me, but you about to get fucked royally. When you find yourself behind bars again, I'm going to make sure I come visit you. My face will be the last one you see before they give your ass the chair. You killed and Spaded your girl, your mama, and your baby. Nigga they gone kill you tomorrow."

Knowing I had the upper hand, I felt on top of the world. Hanging up the phone, I went to change cars. I needed to go to work and I had to find a new place to stay. There was no way I would ever go back to that house. Singing all the way home, I screamed out fuck Spade. His bitch ass got exactly what he deserved. If he had stuck to the plan, none of this would have happened. Now he would live the remainder of his life knowing he was the cause of his own down fall. Him and his bitch. I hope they both rot in hell. Looking to the sky, I smiled knowing I avenged my baby.

"Shawn I did it son. You can sleep peacefully now. Rest on baby, mama had you." Getting in my car, I changed my clothes right there in the front seat. Heading to work, I smiled at my transformation. As I got out of my car, Tupac came to mind. I ain't no killer but don't push me.

CHAPTER TWENTY FIVE SHVONNE

I was pissed off that the bitch Halle got the drop on me. I barely made it in the door and the bitch used a taser on me. She zapped the fuck out of me and all I felt was my body jerk and fall to the ground. I had slob leaking out of my mouth. The bitch grabbed me by my ankles and dragged me my ass down the stairs like I was a fucking rag doll.

Not being able to take the hits, I passed out. When I came to, the bitch had me tied up. Not thinking she had it in her to do anything more, I was surprised when she began pistol whooping me. Since I've known her, she was weak as hell and let a motherfucker run all over her. Bitch ain't never stood up for herself, now the bitch in here trying to kill me over some dick.

They say good dick will make you say fuck your own life, and that shit was true as fuck. This bitch risking her life over a nigga that didn't give a fuck about her. Before I could shake my head and finish what the hell I was thinking, she beat the thoughts out of my ass. I knew it wouldn't be long before I passed out again. This bitch must have had a lot of anger built up. Her hoe ass Spaded me while I was looking her dead in her eyes. Not being able to help it, I screamed out in pain. That shit hurt worse than labor. She dug with a passion, and I cried until after she was done. Even Spade was considerate enough to do the shit after a motherfucker was dead.

This bitch was a different kind of monster. My ass was barely awake when Spade came in. After he got the info out of the bitch, we got the fuck up out of there. I felt weak, but I needed to know what was going on with Jelly. Hearing Spade talk to the bitch that had my child, my blood started boiling. All this time he was blaming me, but the shit was about him.

"You telling me your bitch mad you left her alone and kidnapped my baby. This entire time, you tried to make it seem like it was me. You're the reason for all this shit. Halle was a tool used by your bitch." The nigga looked at me and laughed and I slapped the curls off his ass. Looking like Big Red when he dangled Bird from the balcony. My office hours are from?

"You don't even know what the fuck you talking about. Everything that happened to you is because of your ass. She is a State's Attorney and you killed her son. She came to me because she wanted your ass dead and she knew I had a vendetta against you. The bitch mad because I didn't kill your ass. I broke our deal." If I wasn't looking ugly as shit, he would see my face expression was saying aww.

"I'm sorry. I'm just going crazy because of my baby. She is going to kill them. Spade, you need to do something. Can you pay somebody to find them?"

"By the time I do that, they will be dead." His phone rung and we saw it was his mama. That nigga damn near broke his finger trying to answer.

"Ma, where are you? You good?"

"Hell naw I ain't good. That bitch got me locked up somewhere."

"How the fuck you let her get the drop on you. Your ass been in the streets all your life. What happened to all that tough ass shit. Fuck." Spade was pissed, but he was taking it out on his mama for no reason.

"Nigga, she knocked me the fuck out. That's how. I didn't even make it in the door all the way. When I woke up, I was locked in a room with Jelly. My whole right side hurt. Bitch got my wig loose and I have a headache out of this world."

"Ma, I need you to try and figure out where you are. She plans on killing y'all and framing me. I can't come to you if you don't know where you are. Is it the address I sent you to?"

"Nigga you better come find me. Gone send my ass out here knowing I'm old and shit. Your ass got the easy job. Pebbles ass probably already handled it and you just picked her up. Shame on you for sending an old ass lady to do your job." Ms. Janice ass talked all that shit before we left, now she talking about old lady.

"Ma, I don't know how much time we got. I need you to find out where you are."

"How the fuck am I supposed to know. I'm locked in a room."

"My room." Me and Spade looked at each other.

"Jelly, are you in your room?" I screamed through the phone.

"My room mommy." Trying to make sure she wasn't confused, I started questioning Ms. Janice.

"What color are the walls? Is her bed Pink? On the wall do it say the world is yours and I'm going to give it to you?"

"Damn, let me answer the first question. The walls are purple and yes to everything else." They were in my house. She underestimated Jelly and that is what just saved their life.

"Ma, we know where you are. We on the way. Call me if the bitch come back. Even if you can't say anything."

"Nigga we all know where we are obviously. In Jelly's room. Hurry up and bring your dumb ass here to get me. I swear you don't have no common sense." He hung up the phone and we drove as fast as we could to my house.

"After we leave here, I'm taking your ass to the hospital. You're not about to die on my watch. I will make sure Jelly is safe and that bitch is handled. You have to get checked out, or you won't even be here for Jelly." Knowing he was right, I nodded. I trusted him to make sure she was good. Hell, he been keeping me alive since he been out, and he was supposed to kill me. It's funny how things worked out sometimes.

"Okay. Just hurry up and get to her." It took us no time to get to them. Instead of Jelly running to me, she ran to Spade. My baby probably didn't recognize me.

"Daddy." Picking her up, he carried her to the car and we followed behind them.

"Pebbles, I thought that bitch fucked me up, but damn. You could have bit her or something. Why you didn't fight back baby? I know it hurt, but you could have did something. You look like you didn't even roll your eyes at her." Laughing, I was in too much pain to be offended.

"You should see her. I'm sure she would rather be in my shoes."

"Don't try to take my son's credit. You know your ass ain't did shit. You can't even see out of your eye. One half closed and the other one trying to Ju Ju on that beat."

"Fuck you. Let's go, I need to go get checked out." Holding each other up, we walked to the car and got in. Tragedy brought us together and I was happy for that. She was great to my daughter, and once I figured out her character, I even learned to laugh at her jokes.

She was a shit talker, but she didn't mean any harm. Once I got out my feelings, I found her to be funny as hell. Spade drove me

154

to the hospital, and I couldn't wait to get in that bed. Halle beat the fuck out of my ass.

CHAPTER TWENTY SIX SPADE

Words can't express how I felt when my baby called me daddy and ran to my arms. That feeling was like no other. I don't see how niggas can go years without seeing their seed. Just to see a smile on her face melted my ass all the way down. She was genuinely excited, and that touched a nigga.

Driving to the hospital, a nigga was in deep thought. Almost losing them put a lot of things into perspective for me. My lil family meant more to me than I cared to admit. Looking over at Pebbles, I was pissed the fuck off with how Halle did her face. She looked like shredded chicken on one side.

Getting out, I went and got a wheel chair and took her inside. After explaining that she was robbed, they took her in the back. I knew I had some business to handle, so I had to leave them here.

"Ma, I have to go find this bitch. I need you to stay with Pebbles and call me if anything goes wrong. Keep an eye on Jelly for me too. Don't let shit happen to them. You got your ass whooped last time, you better win this one or I'm gone clown you." Her head whipped around, and I fell out laughing.

"I'm old, at least I have a reason. Your girl supposed to be tough, but she in there looking like Tyson tried to take her pussy. Boy bye. Go handle that bitch and slap her ass in the head for me.

Funky ass hoe got my ears ringing. I told you not to trust her ass. Now you got your mama sitting in here with a well whooped ass and a twisted wig."

"Just do what I asked, damn. You always gotta be extra. I'll be back as soon as I'm done." Leaving her there laughing at her own jokes, I jumped in my car with murder on my mind. Heading to my stash house, I grabbed some tools and jumped in a burner car that I kept there. I'm sure she wouldn't go back home, so I would have to catch her at work. This would be tricky, but I had no choice but to pull it off.

Pulling into the garage, I drove around until I found her car. Parking next to it, I waited patiently. It took her three hours to come out, but as amped as I was, it only felt like five minutes. As soon as she walked up, I got out with my gun pointed at her. She knew it was over for her.

"You not that fucking bold. They will have your ass surrounded in seconds if you kill me here. You don't intimidate me, get the fuck out of my face." This bitch was cocky as fuck when it came to her work place. She didn't know me at all. I already made sure it was no cameras over here. We were about to have a lil fun.

"Bitch you should have done your research before you set a nigga like me free. The last thing you should have done was open the cage on an animal." Not even giving her a chance at a rebuttal, I pulled the trigger. Thankful for a silencer, I would be able to do what I wanted without drawing attention.

****

Walking in the hospital, I stopped at the desk to find out where they had Shvonne. My moms and Jelly weren't in the waiting room, so I knew they had to have gone to the back. After getting her room number, I walked in with a smile on my face. They had cleaned her up, and her wounds looked better. I wasn't worried about her face. As soon as she was ready, I would send her to a plastic surgeon to get it fixed. Jelly looked happy and content.

"Did you get that bitch? It don't look like you did shit but fix your edges. How the hell your hair get laid and shit and you supposed to been handling business." This was why I only did my mama in doses. She didn't know when to shut the fuck up.

"Ms. Janice, no matter what that nigga do he gone fix his hair after. He's one of them millennial ass niggas."

"Aww son, if you were a metrosexual why you didn't tell me. That explains a lot. You not gay, you just in touch with your feminine side. Baby, I thought you was going to bring home a nigga one of these ye ars."

"Anyway, yeah I got the bitch. Hold on, I'm sure you can see it for yourself." Turning the TV, I found a news station. It was already breaking news.

"Colleagues say they found pieces of State's Attorney Valencia Brolen all over the parking garage. There were no cameras and they stated she had no enemies. Here is an emotional plea from The District Attorney.

"If anyone knows anything, please come forward. Valencia was loved by everyone here. She was the sweetest person here and didn't deserve to die that way. Nobody deserves to die that way. It is a monster on the loose, and I'm begging you to help us find them." Reports states, she was identified from the body parts left behind. Her head was left on the hood of her car. This is breaking news and we will come back to you when we have more details."

My mama looked at me like I had lost my mind. She had never asked what I did, and I never told her any details of how I did my shit. Even though I would want to keep this part of my life from her, she needed to know they were safe and no one was coming after them.

"What the fuck is wrong with you son? Why would you do that? You could have just shot the bitch and hit her a few times for me. You need to be evaluated." Laughing, I didn't respond. Climbing in bed with Shvonne, I pulled Jelly in with us. This was what it was all about. Family. I would protect them at all costs, no matter who the enemy was.

"Does that mean you two finally about to get back together?" My mama was nosy as hell.

159

"Shvonne, I'm not saying the shit is going to be easy, but we can try. I'm dealing with some trust issues with you, but I promise to try and work through them. I'm willing to do that for my daughter, but if you even blink at me too long, I will kill you." Shvonne and my moms slapped me at the same time and I was ready to back hand they asses.

"Don't talk to me like that. I know I fucked up, but you not gone hold that shit over my head. Either you all in or you can walk the fuck away. Either way, I will allow you to see Jelly. Don't get this shit twisted, I'm not pressed for you to be with me." Moms was happy and shit like this girl didn't try to set me up and my feelings wasn't valid.

"Your ass ain't going nowhere but to that fucking basement if you keep talking to me like that. Try me if you want to. All I can do is try, but I will give it one hundred percent."

"You better, or you gone have to watch another nigga with me. You know you can't take it. I know that was you that killed Hanz."

"Fuck yeah I did. Y'all had me fucked up thinking y'all was about to be some happy family. Just know, that's the fate of any nigga that come around your ass. Speaking of, I found out who killed Tiana. I made Valencia tell me." She looked at me like she was waiting on an answer.

"Who?"

"I'll tell you when you are better. Worry about you right now. We have plenty of time. Just know, they aren't a threat."

Leaning over, she kissed me. I wanted to tell dude to back up, she was ugly as shit, but I kissed her back. I loved her ass, and I was no longer in denial.

CHAPTER TWENTY SEVEN SHVONNE

Being home from the hospital was refreshing. I was tired of being laid up in that place. I needed to relax in the comforts of my home. Since Spade's house was the safest, we all went back there. Even his mama. We needed time to heal and doing it together was the best way. All of us needed each other. It was so much that had been done, it was going to take time. I can honestly say Spade was trying.

Every day, he would rub ointment on my face and other wounds. He made sure to tell me I was pretty, so I wouldn't end up feeling self conscience. He even massaged me every hour because my body would hurt. That funky bitch fucked me up, but Spade was trying to get me back to normal. I barely came out of the room. His ass did everything. Jelly was in love with the big ass house, and they were the absolute cutest together.

"Baby, moms took Jelly to her house. I wanted to give you a special night and you know Jelly was going to find me. No matter how big this motherfucker was." My baby came and picked me up, and the shit hurt so bad I punched him in the jaw.

"Can you be gentle damn. You know I'm in pain witcho uglass." Laughing, he carried me into the bathroom and placed me in the jacuzzi. The shit felt so good, I didn't want to get out. Washing every crevice of my body, Spade took his time with me and made sure I was relaxed. Feeling his hand sliding up my leg, a moan escaped my lips.

"I need this pussy. Can I have some of this pussy Shvonne?" He was whispering, and it gave me goosebumps. If the water wasn't full of water, the shit would be full of my juices. He had me wet as hell and I couldn't wait to feel him inside of me. Picking me up out of the tub, he carried me to the bed. My shit was throbbing just from anticipation.

Grabbing a glass of wine, he took a sip and sucked on my nipples. It must have been good to him because he moaned. My body shook from the cool feeling of the wine. Trailing kisses down my body, he stopped and sucked on my tender places. Dipping my toes in the glass, he sucked them sending a shiver up my fucking body. Waiting to see what he would do next, I moaned as soon as he spread my legs apart. Holding his mouth open under my clit, he poured wine on my shit and caught it. Sucking gently on my shit, I think I came in ten seconds flat. I needed him in the worse way.

"Spade baby put it in." Placing a finger over my lips, he stopped me from begging. Needing some type of action, I started sucking his fingers. I guess that turned him on, because he climbed on top of me and slid it in slowly. Every part of my body ached for him. I needed him, and his ass gave it to me. He tried to be gentle at first, but I kept thrusting my hips against him hard and fast.

"You wanted this dick now take it." My ass damn near had tears in my eyes. I wanted the dick so bad, I forgot my body was sore. Never slowing up, he kept fucking me like we had no more time. My body began to shake, and he stroked that nut right up out of my ass. Spreading my legs into a split, I cringed from the pain. His ass didn't give a fuck. That's why people say be careful what you wish for.

Thirty minutes later and a sore pussy, he came inside of me. My ass was happy as hell, and I was ready to go my ass to sleep. Rolling over on his side, he looked at me and played in my hair.

"This time around, I'm going to do things the right way. We are going to go on dates and learn each other without all the bullshit. I love you, but I need to know you love a nigga back for real. You gave me the greatest gift I could ask for and I plan on showing you how much I appreciate that shit." Listening to him talk, gave me a lot of regrets.

"Even if you don't believe me, I did feel bad after it was done. I'm sorry Jaleel. We are going to be okay because we have love. Whether you believe it or not, I do love your skinny ass."

"Baby, you talking like you thick out here. Out here looking like thuggish ruggish bone, especially when your hair is curly."

"Your ass just like your mama, always talking shit. Can you be serious for one damn second? Just know I'm sorry and I will do my part to make you know that shit."

"You better. Starting with head every day. Ain't no better way to say you're sorry then some good morning, afternoon love, goodnight daddy head." We laughed as he pulled me to him. We weren't where we were supposed to be, but we were getting there. I never thought I would see the day I could love somebody other than Bam, but I could tuck him away in my heart, knowing I did right by him.

Out of all the shit I went through, I found someone else to love me just as much. Even though our road was rocky, we still made it to our destination. Spade was locked down by his hood love, but he found his way back and stole my heart.

EPILOGUE

Shvonne...

Getting off the plane, my ass was hot and aggravated. Spade ass had knocked me up again and here I was in the California heat seven months pregnant. It's been two years since all of the drama unfolded, and we were the perfect couple. After getting plastic surgery done on my face, I had to go through a healing process.

As soon as it was done, Spade proposed. Since we didn't have friends and shit, we went to Aruba and got married. It was just me, him, his mom, and Jelly. My ass was now Mrs. Spade. No matter how many times I look at my ring, I still couldn't believe that shit.

After asking him countless of times, who killed Tiana, he finally told me. Knowing Spade wasn't going to let me be the one to do it, I called Norie and linked back up with her. I explained everything to her, now here we was on the way to his spot. Word around town was he opened a strip club and was now the man. Heading inside, me and Spade went to one table and Norie sat at the next. It didn't take long for Ju to see her. Valencia told Spade that she was following me every day and saw Halle, Bruno, and Ju following us. I have no idea how Ju found Tiana, but he was determined to take her life like he already hadn't done enough. His ass pimped her out, beat her, and gave her HIV. He could have let her live the rest of her life free, but that was too much like right.

His ass should have done his research, because that was something he would have to pay for. Spade didn't want me to do it, but he knew I wouldn't let the shit go. I had to avenge my best friend, and then I would lay my savage down to rest. One last hurrah and Queen P would be done for good. Seeing Ju walk over to Norie, I knew it was hook line and sinker.

"Hey baby girl. You new around here?"

"Yeah, but I see I found what I was looking for." Smiling on the inside, I couldn't wait to fuck this nigga's life up.

THE END…

KEEP UP WITH LATOYA NICOLE

Like my author page on fb @misslatoyanicole

My fb page Latoya Nicole Williams

IG Latoyanicole35

Twitter Latoyanicole35

Snap Chat iamTOYS

Reading group: Toy's House of Books

Email latoyanicole@yahoo.com

⁇

OTHER BOOKS BY LATOYA NICOLE

NO WAY OUT: MEMOIRS OF A HUSTLA'S GIRL

NO WAY OUT 2: RETURN OF A SAVAGE

GANGSTA'S PARADISE

GANGSTA'S PARADISE 2: HOW DEEP IS YOUR LOVE

ADDICTED TO HIS PAIN (STANDALONE)

LOVE AND WAR: A HOOVER GANG AFFAIR

LOVE AND WAR 2: A HOOVER GANG AFFAIR

LOVE AND WAR 3: A HOOVER GANG AFFAIR

LOVE AND WAR 4: A GANGSTA'S LAST RIDE

CREEPING WITH THE ENEMY: A SAVAGE STOLE MY HEART 1-2

I GOTTA BE THE ONE YOU LOVE (STANDALONE)

THE RISE AND FALL OF A CRIME GOD: PHANTOM AND ZARIA'S

STORY

THE RISE AND FALL OF A CRIME GOD 2: PHANTOM AND ZARIA'S

STORY

ON THE 12TH DAY OF CHRISTMAS MY SAVAGE GAVE TO ME

A CRAZY KIND OF LOVE: PHANTOM AND ZARIA

14 REASONS TO LOVE YOU: A LATOYA NICOLE ANTHOLOGY

SHADOW OF A GANGSTA

THAT GUTTA LOVE 1-2

LOCKED DOWN BY HOOD LOVE 1

?

BOOK 22, AND I CAN'T BELIEVE IT. SIX NUMBER ONES, I'M STILL IN

DISBELIEF. YOU GUYS ARE AWESOME, AND I LOVE YOU. THANK

YOU FOR CONTINOUSLY MAKING MY BOOKS A SUCCESS.

WITHOUT YOU THERE IS NO ME. MAKE SURE YOU DOWNLOAD,

SHARE, READ AND REVIEW. MORE BOOKS WILL BE COMING FROM

ME. BE ON THE LOOK OUT. MLPP WE BRINGING THE HEAT.

CPSIA information can be obtained
at www.ICGtesting.com
Printed in the USA
LVHW02s0245170718
584051LV00008B/202/P